STEAM BATH

STEAM BATH
SWEATY GAY EROTICA

EDITED BY
SHANE ALLISON

Published in the United States by Cleis Press, Inc.,
2246 Sixth Street, Berkeley, California 94710.

Printed in the United States.
Cover design: Scott Idleman/Blink
Cover photograph: Jonathan Skow/Getty Images
Text design: Frank Wiedemann

First Edition.
10 9 8 7 6 5 4 3 2 1

Trade paper ISBN: 978-1-57344-932-8
E-book ISBN: 978-1-57344-949-6

Contents

INTRODUCTION

I was sitting in the bookstore café catching up on some reading when I spotted him. It was Steve from the Tallahassee Baths, browsing through the bargain-price shelves. He was not alone. I watched them for several hot minutes. I could tell how they were standing, how Steve kept grazing the young twink with his hand, that they were an item. I hid behind shelves in hopes that Steve wouldn't see me. The fine young thing he was with was smoking hot with a blond buzz cut. He didn't look like the collegiate boys I was used to seeing Steve hook up with at the baths. I watched Steve and his militant boy-toy stroll damn near hand in hand out of the bookstore into the mall. I was sure I would spot him later that night at the baths. I could only hope so anyway, and perhaps Mr. Buzz Cut would tag along, the two of them with swinging dicks in tow.

I was nervous as hell the first time I went to the baths. It not only took guts but a huge set of low-hanging brass ones just to get up the courage to get in my car and drive there. I didn't know if the thought of prancing around with nothing on but a towel between me and a bunch of horned-up, horse-hung strangers was enough to wrack my nerves or just set my loins ablaze. Swinging dicks under towels indeed. The baths were located on the ass-end of town. The anti-queer, anti-same-sex-gender-loving powers that be were in an uproar at first and did everything in their conservative powers to stop a bathhouse from opening its doors when the owner wanted to locate the place smack-dab in the middle of town where college students frolicked. The local politicians and religious outfits made the usual speeches and preaches about gay men preying on children and eternal damnation, so instead of the owner allowing himself to be run out on a rail by the Jesus freaks, he packed up his (sex) toys and broke ground on the first bathhouse in the capital city. I took one look at the place and thought, *This isn't going to last,* but it's been a year now, going on two and the "house of dick," as some of the boys around like to call it, still stands tall—much like Steve's dick the night we hooked up.

So I walked inside with my gym bag and this young punk of a white boy with dreds was standing behind the counter. He asked to see my ID. I was old enough to be his...older brother, yeah, his older brother, but I took it as flattery instead of offense. I try to hold on to my twentysomething looks like a gold doubloon no matter how many gray hairs spike my chin.

I got a quick lesson in the rules and regulations and what not to do in the back before the young punkster sent me on my randy way. My dick was already twitching in my shorts at the sight of naked and half-naked men milling about, ripping off with their eyes the little clothing that hid very little including the hard-on that was raging under my shorts. I plopped down a twenty spot and grabbed an assortment of rubbers as if they were mints and made my way to where the fun and action awaited me. "Enjoy yourself," was all the boy had left to say to me. I gave him some semblance of a smile.

The pungent odor of poppers was like a pimp slap to my face. The other patrons looked at me like I was a stack of all-you-can-eat pancakes. I felt men zeroing in on my dick and on my ass as I went to change. Most of the men were middle-aged beauts while the rest were silver daddies with dawning beer bellies and ring fingers missing the wedding rings. I changed in one of the locker rooms. I threw my bag with my wallet inside in a vacant locker. No one tickled my fancy until I came across Steve. I knew him from cruising for college boys on one of the local campuses, so it was nice to see a familiar face. I cruised him while old men cruised me, fetishizing this black man, judging by the freak-nasty looks they gave. I followed Steve to his room where I was invited inside. The men looked at us in hope that we would want some company, but it wasn't that kind of water and Steve shut the door in their sweat-soaked faces.

He didn't waste any time and flung his towel off his ass and tossed it to the floor with mine quickly following. Steve was the first of the cruisers to witness me naked. I felt him sizing me up. His moustache prickled my top lip as we made out, our dicks rubbing together like lovers. That night we stroked and sucked each other's dicks, indulged in ass-play and sloppy French kisses until we both came with earth-shattering completion.

We ended up hooking up several more times as weeks passed and we returned to the baths, often inviting someone extra into our sexcapades for spice. My encounter with Steve and other men got the gears in my dirty mind turning. It made me think of the steamy incidents that often occur behind the walls and sometimes open doors of steam baths. I set out on a journey to find the best and raunchiest dick-lit I could get my cum-stained hands on that catered to the theme of steam-bath sex. As an editor, the only rule for me is that the writing "burn off the page." If it moves me to take my dick out, then the literature has won me over.

Rob Rosen turns up the heat once again in his new tale, “The Key.” A young detective sets out to investigate the disappearance of a young twink, but finds more than what he ever thought imaginable in Logan Zachary’s “Incubus Steams.” A tattooed bad boy gets taught a “hard” lesson in Eric Del Carlo’s “Steam Punk.” A mind is not the only thing that gets blown in Rafaelito V. Sy’s “Raf’s Journey.” Things get hot and heavy when a college professor and one of his horny students stumble upon a European steam bath in Roscoe Hudson’s “The Chaperones.” Jeff Funk’s “Easy Dick” shows why the guys who are single-minded about sex are more often found at the baths than the bars; T. Hitman’s “The Aqueducts” makes clear this has been true for many centuries. Freak-nastiness is at its best in Heidi Champa’s “Showtime.” There’s sex in the air if not a turned-up ass in Thom Wolf’s “The Changing Man.” C. C. Williams will make you quiver in his tasty new creation, “What I Am For.” Michael Bracken will have you begging for more when you find out what happens in “Relationships.” I can never get enough of Landon Dixon and his story “Saunsational” is no exception. Newcomer T. R. Verten heats things up “Across the Bay.” It’s sex nostalgia at its best in Jimi Goninan’s, “Meanwhile in the Sauna...” Dudes get nasty in Gregory L. Norris’s, “The Gay Dude.” Find out what’s up “Arnie’s Ass” in Troy Storm’s tale of a coworker’s appealing tail. Veteran gay erotica scribe Shaun Levin brings heart-pounding, dick-throbbing raunch in “The Real End of It.” It doesn’t get any better than the hot and arousing erotic scenarios that have arisen from the creative minds of these scribes. So please, enjoy yourself. I did.

Shane Allison
Tallahassee, Florida

ARNIE'S ASS

Troy Storm

"You're drooling."

"What?" My hand shot automatically to my face. "You asshole," I chuckled, "I'm covered in sweat. We're in a steam bath."

"Yeah," the older dude quirked an eyebrow, "but if we were in dry heat your chin would still be wet. You've been drooling over that guy's ass for a good five minutes."

"Busted." I snugged the towel around my slick hips. Damn, I even had an obvious bone. "He's a buddy. Or rather," I amended, "a coworker. We had a really crappy day. I suggested we take a break and come here. I had no idea he was built like..."

Why the hell was I spilling the story of my life to this smart-ass, old guy in a robe, even though he was handsome and seemed to be in pretty good shape. He probably couldn't give a shit one way or the other about Arnie's ass, but he was listening. And seemed to be interested. And I really needed somebody to spill my guts to right now.

And I had spilled 'em. So I shut up.

He gave me another smug grin. "You didn't slide the towel off...?" He indicated Arnie's magnificent naked glutei maximi with a nod of his head.

"No! He just flopped down on his stomach on the top bench and passed right out. Like I said, it was a really, really bad day and...and then the towel just slid off and there was his butt... bare...."

"Mesmerized you."

"Yeah." I wiped my sweat-drenched eyelids with the back of my forefingers. The most beautiful ass I had ever seen. Who the fuck knew?

"Coworker, you say, and you didn't know he had that Adonis backside?"

"Well, obviously I knew he was well built. He dresses really sharp. Great rack. But we've never been naked around each other before."

The old guy nodded. His eyes cruised over my coworker. "You two gay?"

"What? No, hell...well, Arnie's not. I don't think. Me, I'm not particularly committed to being much of anything. At the moment."

"Curious, maybe?" He looked me up and down. I snugged the towel tighter. My bone was even more outstanding. "You must get some kind of action looking as hot as you do. No pun intended," he smiled, glancing around at the steam bath's heated surroundings.

Hell, that was just what I needed to hear. To get some kind of affirmation after being treated like a dog day after day at that damn office and after all the goddammed hours I spent in the gym. If I was a bust at work, at least give me some kind words for all the sweat and strain of trying to look good. Arnie sure as hell never...

"Thanks, I appreciate that," I said. Now it was my turn to give him the once over. "You look like you might be pretty well pulled together, too, under all that terry cloth." I laid it on, though I couldn't actually tell much. But he was really classy looking. Tight skin. Great salt-and-pepper hair. Square jaw. A real captain of industry. "Work out a lot or just damn good genes?"

He chuckled, dropping an easy, appraising look to my bulging towel. "Thanks, I do have good genes. You should have seen my old man. Brick shit house." He shrugged. "I've got a great trainer. Costs a fucking fortune. I need one, now, to keep me motivated. It's work. Don't get...mature," he stated flatly. "But back to the proposition."

"You're propositioning me?"

"I'm propositioning the both of you," he spelled out. "I also have had a fairly rancid morning. Two good-looking guys, both with great butts, I might add, would really help take a load off." He smiled. "Or two. We can start with drinks and go from there. If it doesn't work out, at least I've had some decent company for a while. Deal?"

I was dumbfounded. For how many years had I been at that damned financial factory unnoticed, and now, half...three-quarters naked, some dude was hot for my body...or at least my companionship. I shook Arnie eagerly.

"Man, wake up! We've been picked up," I chortled. "We've been invited to have drinks with this very classy nice man who has had a shitty day, too. C'mon, we can all get sloshed together."

Arnie pushed himself up, blinking. "What the hell?" He noticed he was starkers. "Oh, shit. Sorry about that." Sitting up, he quickly dragged the towel around his midsection, but not before showing a horse-choking half-hard cock. Shit! I thought.

There went my chance with the "mature" dude, whose relaxed face had suddenly brightened considerably.

The captain of industry regained his complacent composure and reached to shake Arnie's hand. "Your friend has agreed to accompany me in my misery. I hope you'll join us."

Arnie leaned in to focus on the guy, his smile fading and his jaw dropping.

"I'll get dressed and meet you in the lobby." The older dude gave me a subtle thumbs-up before disappearing down the corridor.

"Do you know…?" Arnie was still excited.

"Yeah, I know who it looks like," I said, "but what would he be doing here? He could have anybody he wants any time he wants 'em. All those big-balled, captain-type dudes look alike, anyway." I bent my knees and waggled my hands. "Hey, make me look like Michael Douglas, Amelio. This," I acknowledged, "is not a bad make."

"Michael Douglas should be so lucky," Arnie tucked the towel around his slim hips and hopped off the slatted seat. "I'll bet it's him."

It was.

We went to his apartment, all glass and a thousand floors up. Down below, the plebes weren't even ants, just dots. "Call me Jason," he said, acknowledging his identity easily as his man poured us drinks—his man!—and Arnie and I gawked. We were served caviar and a bunch of other afternoon-type snack stuff while we all chattered away like old buddies about the state of the industry, and then as his man was pouring our third round, Jase got down to business.

"Guys, I like to be up front about my dealings. Especially when it comes to sex, as my several ex-wives', and ex-companions' unhappy lawyers will be glad to explain." Out of the corner of my eye I could see Arnie beginning to tense. "I pay well, but I do have a couple of nonnegotiable requests. Nothing kinky, but..."

"You're paying us to have sex with you?"

Oh, damn. Arnie was instantly in high dudgeon, whatever the hell that means, except at that moment it meant I was about to lose a great afternoon of what I knew was going to be great sex with a really terrific captain of industry who was turning out to be one of the coolest rich dudes I had ever met, not that I had met all that many nice, good-looking older dudes no matter how old. Or rich.

"Didn't your friend...?"

"My fucking friend didn't tell me shit! This is disgusting. I thought you were turning out to be a really great guy, but I'm not about to be pimped by anybody for anything!"

He stormed toward the private elevator. "And I guess you're not coming with me, are you...*friend!*"

"Arnie, I...I..." I looked at Jason who looked bereft. I shook my head.

"Arnie," Jason said, placatingly, trying not to plead. "I didn't mean to offend. I just don't want any misunderstandings." The elevator door silently slid shut on an arms-crossed, legs-spread, righteous-looking Arnie. Jeez, he looked hot mad.

I knew whatever was about to happen—if anything was going to happen now—would only last as long as it lasted; I undoubtedly would never get to see Arnie's gorgeous naked ass again; and our longtime friendship that might have ripened into something really great, given time and effort, was at a dismal end.

Jason sighed. He turned to stare out the huge windows for a long moment then, remembering I was still there, said, "You don't have to stay. I understand. A close friendship is important. A couple of hours of sex...are...not as important."

"Well, I've never really had that choice to make before," I said. "I know it's shallow and petty of me, but seems like I should have the couple of hours under my belt before I can make a valid judgment."

Jason tilted his handsome head and studied me for a moment. He grinned, "You really are a slut, aren't you?"

"Takes one, I guess," I grinned back. "I read all those newspaper stories about your various financial...escapades. You really know how to stand your ground. Or rather your lawyers do."

Jason sauntered close. "Is your ass as pretty as Arnie's?"

"Nobody's is. But I bet mine's a lot more fuckable."

"Seems like I should have a couple of hours of trying that out before I can make a valid judgment." His well-manicured fingers closed around my belt as he pulled me into a solid kiss. "Hmm, nice," he pronounced a couple of minutes later. "I like a mouth that's able to handle itself."

"I've got another organ you might want to check out," I purred, yanking somewhat awkwardly at his Brooks Brothers slacks. "Can we get naked in front of these big windows and look down on all we survey?"

"Damn tootin'. Mirrored glass," Jason laughed. "We can see out. They can't see in." He slipped as smoothly out of his clothes as an athlete would suit up. He was pretty much brick-house built like his old man must have been, and he had a dick that put Arnie's horse-choker to shame. Man, this was going to be *fun*! I tore at my jeans and dress shirt like a madman.

"You really are enjoying this, aren't you?" Jason did that tilt of his head thing that made me have to work to peel my jockeys off my petrifying manhood. I nodded, gleefully, and began to dance around the room, naked as the day I was born but with a lot more meat on my bone.

"Now you," I sang. "Let's both jack off onto all those little ninety-nine-percenters scrambling around in the late afternoon gloom miles below us."

"You are a politically incorrect, smug little wanna be ass-kisser with one hot body and a dick that I can't wait to wrap my tonsils around," Jason snorted derisively as he stopped me in flight and pulled my naked backside against his extremely well-taken-care-of front. His big dick dug between my asscheeks and slipped between my legs to nuzzle into my balls. Man, he was huge and getting huger by the minute. My ass ached with the possibilities.

"Fuck me, Jason," I pleaded. "Fuck me in front of everybody." I swept my arms in a big arc, taking in the world outside the mirrored glass. "I want everybody to know you're my man!" I pulled a foil pack from my butthole that I had slid in while I was pulling my clothes off. My little sleight-of-ass delighted Jason. He stretched on the plastic. Then to my amazement he knelt behind and began to eat me out.

"Oh, jeez," I gasped, leaning on the glass, hands spread wide, hoping it was fired to withstand hurricane-force battering. His tongue swirled around in my gaping maw, exciting nerve endings that hadn't been excited since high school. I squealed as he lapped at my balls and stroked his fingers and mouth over my ass and gnawed at my perineum. My whole crotch went off like a string of firecrackers as his strong fingers probed my hole and stretched and stretched until it felt like he could reach right in there and shake hands with my tonsils.

Then with an approving, "Fucking exceptional," he steadied my hips to position himself and fed his cannon inexorably into me. He had barely socketed the horse-cock home when the juice shot out of me in arcing rifle splats, clotting up the view.

"Beauty butt, you unleash one powerful load. Let's see if we can pump a few more globs onto the panes." He pumped his dick in and out of my asshole until I thought my flapping dick was going to burst into flame. More of my stuff burped out of my slapping meat to sling itself both down into the depths of the immaculate wall-to-wall carpet and smack into the heavy drips working their way down the inside of the glass walls.

Jason took a breather, still clamped behind me. Hazily, I looked up, up at the clouds. My ass soared, my nuts fluttered like the gulls gliding by, checking themselves out in the mirrored shaft they circumnavigated. My dick was still rigid, jerking quietly as it ratcheted down, gravity finally draining the last of the heavy drops of cum that jeweled in the intense light.

Throbbing, mature meat filled my rectum, pressing against the sides of the clutching sheath. I did the squeezing now, molding the captain's butt plug, kneading it to keep fucking. "Keep at it, old man," I begged. "Cream my hole. Load me up with that aged nectar."

Jason's well-toned body pounded against mine unmercifully. Suddenly he tensed and gasped. "Thank you, thank you, thank you..." as his cream whizzed up my butt, packing the condom. He hung on for dear life. His hips jerked and his dick fired and fired until he was empty.

The gasping older dude buried his head in the nape of my neck and sighed deeply as his pounding chest slowed. "Beautiful, man, beautiful. I was afraid I might not make it. I forgot to down my little blue pill. But that vacuum butt of yours kept me hard and pulled it right out of me. We could sure as hell use you in our sales department. I'm afraid we won't get much further than this." He was already beginning to deflate. "Sorry."

"Hold onto my tits," I said, firmly. "Snuggle against me. I want to feel every inch of you, inside and out. Damn, if Arnie were here, we could make a hot sandwich of you, and then I betcha your big ole dick would stay hard as a fuckin'...fuck stick, uh, pole...*rod*!"

He chuckled, his personal-trainer-honed biceps tightening around my chest. "Pure poetry," he purred. His smooth palms rotated over my stiff nubs. "You do know how to make a guy feel like a fairly decent piece of meat." His hips tilted back as he pulled his softened dick slowly out of me, savoring the stripping squeeze I was putting on him. "God, that's nice," he murmured, as he continued to evacuate. "You have a very talented tunnel there, young man. And very nice nips. And, as you noted, truly fuckable buttcheeks."

"Not as fuckable as Arnie's." I looked down. Somewhere among those dots was a disgruntled perfect butt, attached to a really nice guy: a lonesome, lost soul grimly stalking through the canyons, back to the horrific grind, knowing he had kept his precious morals intact, never to be tempted by me again. All because Mr. Captain of Industry had offered to pay. Hell, paying is what we all do, one way or other.

Jason's hand played over my front, lightly kneading, fingertips gently tracing, as he leaned against me, his well-honed torso and thighs molding against my backside. "How long have you been working on him?" He blew gently into my ear and lightly tongued the outer shell.

"Couple of years." My eyes closed and I let the guy work his magic. My dick was still rock, gently swaying, but there were a few empty little corners inside that needed to be filled and his filler had been a masterpiece. What the hell, the damn office could wait. I needed Jason's dick up my ass, again. I needed my dick down his throat, his hands wrapped comfortingly around my nuts, squeezing the seed out of them. I needed his guts glugging down my cream. I needed to be fucked... I ached to fuck...

"Arnie," Jason said, gnawing on the nape of my neck, "might come back if we ask nicely." He gently ground his groin into my butt. Even detumescent, his formidable meat spread my asscheeks. "If you're really serious about that sandwich thing." A quiver ran though his body. "What's his cell number?"

"He's straight," I whined. "And he's got some sort of moral hang-up about...I don't know...gays...or gaydom...or...."

"Yeah, right." Jason punched the number I intoned. He was still plastered against me. I was still bracing myself on the huge windows. The gulls were still circling.

"Arnie? Jason. Sorry about the money thing." Jason pulled off, shook himself and started pacing the pristine wall-to-wall. He was in Negotiating Mode. He seemed almost as jacked as when he was fucking my ass. "You want to give that beautiful butt of yours away, fine with me. Your buddy and I have just had a superior session. Released a lot of tension. You want to join us for the second round? He's dumping the rest of the workday. We'll have a few bites, a couple of drinks, then see who drops from exhaustion first. Interested?" He listened a few seconds. "Yeah." He turned the phone over to me.

"Are you crazy?" Arnie was in high dudgeon...or whatever. "We've got to get back to work. You can't let all that money and all that...."

"Where are you?"

"What!"

"Where the fuck are you, Arnie?"

"Uh...I'm...I'm in front of the building. I, uh, thought you might be coming out. Eventually."

"Right. Come on up."

"What?"

Suddenly a lot of murky stuff became clear. It must have been the height; the purity of the oxygen up there. Arnie had not stomped off to work in high dudgeon, pure and untainted by the offer of money for sex. He was waiting around. For me to stomp off, too, and prove to himself he had made the right decision. *Or for something else.*

Earlier, he had not accepted my invitation to one of the financial district's most notorious steam baths unaware of what might happen. He knew damn well what might happen and he wanted something to happen. He wanted to make his stand and be stood down. He wanted for something to happen that was different from the shit he and I and a hell of a lot of other plebes had been enduring for months, years. He wanted to blow his load. To clean out his pipes. To start over.

Neither one of us could have possibly expected it to be one of the one-percenters who would give us that opportunity, but Jason seemed pretty decent. He was certainly in great shape and he admired what we had to offer: my enthusiasm, Arnie's ass. Arnie was no fool. He had made his stand and we had called him on it. "Will you guys come back to the steam bath?"

I motioned Jason over. We both listened. "We could rent a private room. I feel kinda out of my element up there, you know? I gotta kind of take it slow. You think Jason would mind?"

"Mind a free fuck?" Jason said into the phone. "Free blow jobs? Free eating out of an ass even my very expensive trainer would bite his knuckles over? Meet us in Room Twelve. Be ready."

"How do you know it'll be available?"

"Tell Pete at the desk that Jase said you're expected. It'll be available."

We met him in Room 12. The Captain's Suite. Arnie was naked and nervous. The sweat was pouring and not just from the steam bath. And half-hard. I almost passed out he was so beautiful. He opened his mouth.

Jason put a finger on his open lips. "Don't say anything. You've got a buddy here who needs dibs on what part of you he gets first. Okay?"

Arnie's big eyes cut toward me. "Uh...sure."

The corner of Jason's mouth crooked up. "Heads or tails?"

I smiled, unzipping my pants. "Tails."

THE REAL END OF IT

Shaun Levin

Around the 12th of June 1999 I fell in love. The kind of love that is so desperate and so new—and by new I mean archetypal in a way that you hadn't felt since childhood—so intense that every disappearance of the beloved, whether he's going back to his flat to sleep, or, in my case, to his girlfriend—this going away was akin to death, a kind of nullification of my existence. Two things rescued me from falling to pieces—and when I say "falling to pieces" I mean a sense that you might never stop waiting, that I had the capacity to wait for hours on end—like being left in a cot, or losing sight of that familiar face in the supermarket when you are a boy and suddenly realize you are alone in the universe. The kind of abandonment that makes you dread you will never recover. Poetry and painting made survival possible—and they made it possible by making sense of these feelings—or rather they provided these feelings with something to hold on to—it was how I wrote my first book.

So yes, for a while during those months before and after the millennium Martin and I were in love. It ended badly—not in a tragic or violent way, but more as a kind of fizzling out, so incongruous with how it all began and the months of our great and profound love. We'd reached a dead end. He was still living with his girlfriend and had no intention of leaving her. I was slowly pulling myself out from under the avalanche that was our affair and regaining my self-respect, which, ironically, had been built up by his love. I was disappointed; I wanted more and I wasn't going to get it. So I left.

We didn't see each other for a long time after that. Two years, perhaps. It's all a bit vague, that period of not seeing him. Mainly I just got on with my life in a haze of grief and recovery. I dated. I turned forty. I had a boyfriend for a while, a man named Greg who lived in Ealing, on the other side of London ("in the suburbs," I joked). We spent alternate weekends at each other's place. They were calm days, those days with Greg, none of the high drama of jealousy and infatuation and my constant state of clinging that had characterized my time with Martin.

I started going to the sauna, and on my second or third visit I bumped into Martin. It became a ritual after that, as much as you can call meeting up with someone for sex every six months a ritual. Recently, I'd planned to go to the sauna after a conference in Mile End, only a ten-minute cycle ride away. By coincidence, though no big surprise, for it had happened several times before over the past few years—I'd think of texting or calling to see if he wanted to meet up, and a preemptive text would come through from him. Just a couple of hours before I left the house for the conference, Martin called to see if I wanted to meet up.

"When did you get back from New York?" I said.

"This morning."

He was horny, he said. He hadn't had sex in over a month,

and to top it all off he'd just been made redundant. Did I want to get together?

"I was planning to be there around four thirty," I said.

"I'll leave work early," he said. "But I have to be home for dinner."

We are naked in a cubicle. There's a faint whiff of shit in the air, as if some guy's just been fucked, or maybe there's been an accident. Whatever the story, the air is full of poo. It's repellent, as if the smell were a room in itself, as if you'd entered an altered space—the way the scent of a certain aftershave can transport you. The smell of shit is unnerving, a case of the profoundly intimate in a public space. Aftershave aims for the opposite effect.

"You're not wearing Davidoff's Cool Water," I say.

"I've still got a bottle at home," Martin says.

I want to say that I don't like the scent he's wearing now, that the hint of apple is turning me off. Apples, I want to say, are for pies and fruit salads. But I don't say anything because I want to be here in the cubicle with him. So few of the men I end up having sex with, or bring home, or invite over—none, really—are bulkier than me. But Martin is. He is broader and heavier, and even as I have increased in size through enthusiastic gym-going, he has put on weight through comfort and discontent. He's in a sexless relationship with a man quite a few years older than him (yes, he came out of the closet) and he's been working in a job he hates, a City job where they make you feel bad for going home before ten at night.

He is still handsome. But his arse is bigger.

And when he speaks, I notice a slight stale odor from his mouth, breath that smells unwashed, like something inside him (his liver?) is not quite right. It's like a secret, like noticing that Julie Andrews, or the Queen, perhaps, has circles of sweat under her arms as she puts out her hand to greet a subject, a minor shortcoming that resonates with the force of a major deficiency and casts a shadow over one's faith.

It can be that dramatic.

He plays absentmindedly with his cock while we talk, tweaks my nipples, says how much he misses this—my hairy chest—and repeats (because he has said this before) that I taught him everything he knows about sex.

"I was innocent when I met you," he says.

"Innocent?" I say. "You're full of shit."

"It's true," he says.

"You've always been a slut," I say.

"Yes," he says. "But I wasn't very good at it."

I move to lie on top of him, and his concise, sharp penis jabs into me. My cock is soft between us. I want to feel passion, to have everything we've had fill my body again, to be consumed by desire, maddened by it. I have never felt that kind of desire, the desire I felt for him, for any other man, not before and not since. But I realize, though I could be wrong, that the desire had little to do with him; it was my rebirth into the world, the result of my father's death, and the devastation and the liberation a loss like that brings with it.

"So," he says. "What would turn you on now?"

"I don't know," I say, because what I should be doing is getting up and walking away, and if not that, telling him that what I really want is to lie here and be stroked, to nestle my head into the vast mass of his smooth chest.

"How about we find a guy," he says. "I'll fuck him while he sucks you off?"

"Sure," I say.

"Would you like that?" he says.

"I could get into it," I say.

We wrap our towels around our waists and head back out into the corridor.

"You go that way," I say. "We'll report back in five."

I head for the dark room at the end of the corridor; it's a pair of rooms with a brief antechamber between them. The large room has a raised mattress in the middle that could fit about ten people; there's enough space around the platform for people to walk in twos, but they walk alone, solitary perambulators on the dark path around the camomile patch. The smaller room has four open booths, two on each side, a glory hole between each pair. Like confessionals, but without the privacy. A man I know is standing in the antechamber. He and I have fooled around here a couple of times. We have friends in common on the queer arts scene, though we never seem to bump into each other at events or exhibitions; we keep our sex to the confines of the steam room. His name is Alex. We stand and talk and Martin passes us every now and then, in his back-and-forth searches. With Alex, I feel like we're parents in a playground, our minds halfheartedly on the conversation, our eyes on the whereabouts of our children.

"A big mistake," I tell Alex.

"Is he the one?" he says.

"Which one?" I say.

"From your book of love and recipes," Alex says.

"He is," I say. "But he's changed."

"Or you have," he says.

"Do you think he's cute?" I say.

"I could get into him," Alex says. "Quite easily."

The three of us kiss, our mouths a wet sloppy confusion; more than one tongue in my mouth, and I can't detect which is mine. It's sexy in a nice way, but I'm not hard. I'm not sure why I'm doing this, why I'm here, but I feel I have to be, that it's right, that I'm exorcising something: disgust as a way to rid myself of this old love. Alex is gentle and tentative. He's a couple of inches taller than Martin and me, so he bends down to keep our heads level. He's tall and skinny, but there's something solid about him, like a tree trunk, and there's a moment when he and Martin kiss and I rest my head against his shoulder, a smooth bony silver birch of a shoulder, and press into him. We don't talk. We sweat a lot and it pools on the floor around us, slippery on the black lino. And then while Alex and I are kissing, Martin goes behind him and puts a condom on and slides into him. Effortlessly. And Alex pushes back into him and gradually moves his torso down, like a crane, until his mouth is level with my middle and I can feed him my cock.

Martin fucks in quick jerks, nothing gentle, just a kind of repetitive thrust, and I look at him, this man I was in love with for such a long time, when I wanted nothing else in the world, only him.... I would have betrayed my family, abandoned friends, I really would have, and now all he is is this: an unhappy, overweight man fucking a sweet guy called Alex who plays the piano and teaches music to primary-school kids and just wants us all to have a good time. And I think, as I look into Martin's face: *This is the moment when I should be smiling at you; we should be looking at each other with delight over the back of a handsome man who is giving us pleasure with his arse and mouth,* but I cannot. I cannot smile. All I can think is: *Who are you? How can it be that I feel nothing for you?*

I slide back and forth in Alex's warm mouth and stroke his soft thick hair and touch his cheeks and Martin is about to come, intensely, eagerly and selfishly.

And then it's over.

Martin pulls his cock out and Alex straightens up, his body

firm between us. I press my chest against Alex's, put my arms around him and we keep kissing, keep playing with each other's cock, pinching each other's nipples, smiling and making sounds of pleasure. Martin points at his watch and does the I-better-not-be-late face and I give him a small wave and he does the same, a wave I'm familiar with, that cautious echo of a much bigger gesture, and he unlocks the cubicle door and leaves and I close it again and lock it and go back to Alex and that is it between Martin and me. That really is and was the end.

"Very efficient, your muse," Alex says.

"Enough about him," I say. "Enough."

THE KEY

Rob Rosen

I spotted it on the floor by his desk. A key, gold, on a small chain, the tag with the word RAIN printed across it. It must've fallen out of his front pocket. I hurried over and picked it up, rubbing the silver tag in between my fingers. "I wonder what you unlock," I whispered to myself before tossing it back down.

Brad returned a short while later. I watched him from my cubicle. He quickly scooped the key up off the floor, looking around to see if anyone else had spotted it, the slightest patch of red washing across his stubbled cheeks. I looked away, pretending to be working. This was a ritual of mine, in fact. I'd often stare at him from across our office, fantasizing about what he looked like out of those Brooks Brothers suits of his, my cock throbbing at the very thought of it.

And then I typed in R-A-I-N plus my city into Google. *Bingo*, I thought, that throbbing cock of mine going full-on tree-limb hard and thick. Because, surprise, surprise, the place was a local bathhouse, exclusive, membership required. Not an establishment I pictured Brad hanging out in, especially since I wasn't even sure that he was gay. Still, it did put a rather twisted thought in my rather twisted head.

Maybe, I figured, I could make those fantasies of mine a reality after all.

First things first, though. I called the club up and asked if I could join. Turns out, I could, if I wanted to fork up some major do-re-mi dough for an annual membership. "What about if I'm a referral?" I asked.

"Depends. Who's the referral from?" the guy on the other end asked.

"Brad Stanley," I replied, prodding at the tenting in my slacks.

"Twenty percent off then," he told me.

"What about for a month, just to test it out?" I tried.

He paused. "Drop by on Saturday after eight. Freebie. If you like it, you pay for the year. Best I can offer."

I gave him my name and told him I'd be there, a bead of sweat suddenly forming on my brow before it came trickling down my cheek. I hung up the phone. I was a man suddenly on a mission. Now I just needed to put the rest of my plan into action. And pray that it'd work.

Seems my prayers were answered, too. And pretty quickly, I might add. See, my office had its weekly meeting about thirty minutes later. Everyone included. Mandatory. Me, I waited to go in last, hands trembling as I walked past his desk, to his coatrack. Inside his jacket my fingers slunk, the cool leather in my grip. Heart racing now, I opened up his wallet and took out a credit card, the one that was three back, figuring it wasn't the one he used most often. I pocketed the card, put the wallet back where I found it, and hightailed it to the meeting. Just like that, easy as pie.

Then all I had to do was call Brad's cell, later that day, when he wasn't at his desk. I did it from a private conference room, waiting until I was alone in there, stroking my cock as I dialed. The sound of his recorded voice made my balls rise. "Mister Stanley," I said, voice disguised, "this is the manager at RAIN. We found your Visa card in one of the lockers. I'm off tonight, and managers must return lost items. I'll be at the club tomorrow night, Saturday, after eight. Please drop by to pick it up then." Click went my phone, just as I shot my load, a thick wad of come that filled my upturned palm. *Please take the bait, Brad. Please.*

Turns out, he took it. Hook, line, and sinker. Plus a cock ring and some nipple clamps to boot. Yup, Brad was full of surprises all right.

And I was in for quite a few of them.

The first was the club itself. Sure, I'd been to bathhouses before, but this was a new breed. It was posh and elegant, well worth the obscene annual fee. If you had the money to burn, I mean. Which, clearly, I didn't. Still, at least for one night, it was free, my name at the door, as promised.

The second surprise upon entering was the men. All of them nice looking, under fifty and not a flabby gut in sight. Suddenly, I was glad for my regular morning workouts. No more griping about them for me. Especially once I was handed my towel and my locker key and told that I had to be undressed to walk around, either nude or in the towel, which I opted for. At least for the time being. Then I turned in Brad's credit card, knowing that he'd eventually get it back and be none the wiser as to my shenanigans.

And so, heart beating like a fucking rhythm section, I had a look around.

Place was divided into theme rooms, all large, with men either watching the scenes or taking part. Me, I watched. Watched the two guys getting it on in the back of the cab, the circle jerk on a field of Astroturf—and on the fifty-yard line no less—and the daisy chain in the all-leather room, the smell of it instantly making my cock rigid behind the terry-cloth constraint.

Through room after room I went, until I found the last one, the reason the place was called RAIN.

It was smaller than the other rooms, if only by a little, the floor a grating made out of rubber to allow the water to flow down and out. And flow it did, in a constant shower from the ceiling, bathwater-warm and misting. "Whoa," I managed. "Now *this* is something different."

I hung my towel outside the door and walked in, the water rushing over me, sending a chill down my back despite the warmth. Steam rose from the floor, parting as I made my way farther inside. I stared at the screen in the back of the room, the waterfall video covering the wall, the sound of rushing water and moaning filling my ears. The video would change over time, the room turning from a thunderstorm at sea, to a dripping cave, to a locker room, but the peripheral sound would remain, a constant moan from all sides bouncing off the tiled side walls. That and the water, falling in sheets or barely drizzling, but always present.

And then there he was, Brad, dead center, naked save for the aforementioned cock ring and nipple clamps, which had a chain in between them, his fingers pulling down, eyelids fluttering in apparent rapt delight.

I stopped, frozen to the spot. There was my fantasy suddenly made real. He was naked, belly etched, a thick matting of fur between water-soaked pecs, prick jutting out, steely stiff, balls like full-sized lemons, swaying as he continued to pull on the chain. Adonis, as it turned out, had nothing on Brad.

Then, as if sensing that he was being watched, his eyes popped open.

He froze as well, stock-still, as if on film and the movie projector jammed, only to right itself a heartbeat later. "Steve," was all he said, his hands releasing the chain as the water slowed down to a trickle, the cave scene on now, the room darkening as I moved in closer to him, the sound of bats taking wing filling my ears.

"Gay, huh?" I asked, with a sly grin.

"What gave it away?" he replied, echoing my grin.

I pointed to his prick, which, in turn, pointed right back at me. Then my finger went around the room, to the men sucking each other off, or watching the two of us, to see what would happen next. "Can't get gayer than this," I reasoned.

Then he pointed down to his cock, with a wink, and replied. "Well, you could." Emphasis on *you*. In truth, I preferred his reasoning to mine. Meaning, I closed the gap between us and sunk to my knees, the fat tip of his cock soon inside my mouth, balls nestled in my hand. He reached down and stroked my head as I sucked. "You're wet," he rasped.

I popped his prick out and licked the salty precome off the tip. "That makes two of us." Then I went back to his dick, taking the entirety of it down my throat, gagging with glee as I reached around and clamped on to his stellar ass, my fingers quickly finding the sweet spot, crinkled and nestled in a ring of wet hair. He moaned as he rocked his cock in and out. I moaned as I stroked my billy club of a dick, so hard it could crack open a safe by that point.

I stared up at the endless stretch of muscle and water-slick hair, at the blue veins evident beneath alabaster flesh, at equally blue eyes staring down at me, sparkling beneath the dim lighting. "You always were an overachiever," he said as my mouth finally reached the base of his shaft.

I retracted my lips, his cock springing out in an audible *pop*.

"You ain't seen nothing yet. Just wait until the *slide* show."

He grinned and joined me on the rubber floor, eye to eye now, dick to dick. "Yeah?" he whispered. He pointed to the others watching us. "I see the show; where's the slide?"

I moved in, his lips on mine as the water poured down and over, a torrent to a trickle and back again, all while I gently pulled down on the nipple clamps, his moans pushing out of his lungs and down my throat, body rumbling like the piped-in thunder. "Get on all fours," I told him, "and I'll show you the slide part."

His smile lit up the otherwise darkened room as another crack of thunder boomed overhead, a sudden bolt of lightning illuminating his naked, wet body. Another crack, another bolt, and he was on his hands and knees, ass jutting out as the storm began to break. Apt that the clouds parted just as his cheeks did, his asshole winking out at me as bursts of sunlight poked through and illuminated the ceiling.

The rain turned to mist again as I dove in like a man who hadn't eaten in days, devouring his hole, licking and biting it as I yanked on his heavy nuts, his spine arching with each tug. I pulled back an inch to stare at it all, to forever etch the vision of his ass and hole into my memory, as the rainbow's arc beamed itself across the ceiling. "Is there a pot of gold hidden in there?" I couldn't help but ask.

He craned his neck around and grinned. "Maybe not a pot, but it wouldn't hurt to check."

And so I went diving for gold, one slick finger slid in and up and back, his moan ricocheting around the room, the watchers on the sidelines echoing the sound as the rain again began to drizzle and mist, the walls transforming into sheets of waterfalls on all sides, surrounding our little lake of inequity. And then a second finger joined the search, both digits swirling inside of him as he started a slow stroke on his dick, balls swaying with each shove of my wrist. The third finger seemed to do the trick, though, as the mist picked up all around us, a blanket of fog that rolled over his body as the triple assault continued on his ass. "Maybe I should try a different tool," I shouted above the waterfall's din.

Just then, a rubber got tossed our way. Brad reached over and grabbed it and handed it back as he flipped over, my fingers retracting from his rump. He winked up at me again as he watched me slide that sucker on. "If you can't find the gold, Steve, maybe there will be a silver lining in the end," he said, shaking his limb of a prick at me.

I spit in my hand, lubed us up as best I could, considering how drenched we both were, and slid my prick inside of him in one even glide. I moaned. My face tilted up to the clouded ceiling. "Mmm," I hummed, as a million volts of electricity shot up my back. "And what a nice lining it is." Then I stared down at him as he contentedly pumped his prick. "Now enough of the witty repartee and double entendres, Brad; time for you to get fucked."

"Amen," said a faceless voice from the side; everything was blanketed in a sea of mist and fog by that point.

Brad chuckled, the sound like seashells being tossed at the shoreline. Then again, that might've actually been the sound I heard, the scene changing yet again, rolling waves now surrounding us, a spray of water hitting us, seagulls flying overhead, sailboats off in the distance. You couldn't ask for a nicer setting to get your rocks off to.

I slid my cock out, the beast floating midair before it was crammed back inside, with a grunt from Brad and then one from me, moans all around as the waves kept crashing. Out and in, slow at first, but picking up speed as every nerve ending in my body set off sparks. The sea grew rough, and then so did I, twisting his clamped nipples and slapping his chest as I piston-fucked his ass.

"Close," he panted up at me, water dripping off his face, eyes glazed over.

"Closer," I groaned back, slamming my cock up inside him, until my balls lapped up against his ass and my body began to quake and tremble just as I exploded inside of him, filling that rubber up with a steady stream of come. He came a split second later, my eyes glued to his massive prick as it twitched and then shot, his body writhing on the rubber grating as gooey beads of come flew this way and that, the watchers coming right along with us, our collective moans even louder than the churning ocean that surrounded us.

I pulled out and collapsed on top of him, our lips again meshed together, a deep soulful kiss that stretched on out to the horizon in front of us. I watched as the sunset began to settle over us, the room turning golden as the rain and mist at last began to subside. "I'm waterlogged," I admitted, when our mouths separated.

Again he chuckled. "I won't need a shower for the rest of the year, I think."

I hopped up and then helped him do the same. Then we beat a hasty retreat, so that the next revelers could have their turn. I turned to look at him as we walked back to the locker room, oddly embarrassed at seeing him naked in the glaring hallway lights. He glanced my way and responded with a sheepish grin.

"Nice place," I said.

He shrugged. "The owner's a friend of mine."

I nodded. "That explains how you can afford it."

Another shrug, another glorious smile. "Worth it for that

room though, huh? Their water bills must be through the roof."

And then we went to our lockers and got dressed before heading for the front door. We were stopped by the manager just before we exited. "We found your Visa, Mister Stanley," he said, handing over the plastic card.

"Oh, yeah, right," Brad said, sliding it inside the now-familiar wallet.

Then we walked outside, the cool night air hitting our faces. I turned to look at him and him at me. Then, in unison, we both said, "I have a confession to make."

I paused, stunned at hearing my words coming out of his mouth. "You first," I said.

He nodded and grinned, a flash of red up his neck that was evident beneath the silver glow of the moon. The real one this time, not the one we'd left in the rain room. "I, uh, well, you see, I dropped the key the other day on purpose."

"Huh?" I squeaked out, heart again racing.

"The key," he said, pulling it from his pocket, the gold glinting in his hand. "It's for members. And I was, um, hoping you'd pick it up when I dropped it." His blush reddened. "I showed up tonight, praying you'd do the same." His grin widened. "Now, what was your confession?"

My blush matched his, though I only gave him half the story. "I, um, I watch you at work, from across the office." I laughed, nervously. "A lot."

He reached out and pulled me in to him. "Duh, Steve. You're a bit obvious, you know."

"Go figure," I replied, my lips brushing his. "That okay with you?"

He nodded and brushed right on back. "I dropped the key, didn't I?" Then he reached into his pocket and pulled out yet another one.

"What's that one for?" I asked, my hand stroking his lower back.

"My apartment. Want to come over?"

I nodded and pulled him in even tighter. "Yup," I replied. "Only, no showers, okay? Heck, don't even offer me a glass of water; I think I've had enough of it for a while."

"Sounds like a plan," he said, as we walked arm in arm down the sidewalk.

I grinned knowingly at the word.

And oh what a plan it turned out to be.

INCUBUS STEAMS

Logan Zachary

Incubus*—a demon in male form that lies upon sleepers in order to have intercourse with them.*

Third Young Man, Missing!
Another young man has disappeared over the weekend. Jeron Nichols, twenty-two, was last seen Friday night with his friends. His roommate hasn't seen him since...

Detective Timothy Ryan entered the new bathhouse called Incubus Steams. Its tag line read: *Meet the man of your dreams and make all your fantasies come true...* Ryan smiled to himself; it was a bold statement for any place to make, but from a bathhouse in Toronto? He doubted it.

Damon Noir sat at the front desk in the lobby's booth, shirtless. He smiled when he saw Ryan enter. "Good morning and welcome to Incubus Steams."

Ryan scanned Damon's hairy, twenty-two-year-old chest. He noted the black hair and a dark olive complexion; his deep, brown eyes; and an even smile under a small moustache. Ryan reached into his jacket pocket and pulled out his badge. "I'm here to ask you a few questions."

Damon stood up, revealing he was naked sitting in the booth. He had a thick bush of black hair and a thick penis that appeared to be semierect. It rose up and down as Ryan's eyes looked at it.

Ryan startled at the sight and brought his eyes back up to Damon's eyes. He could see the smile inside, knowing he had been caught staring.

"As you can see," Damon spread his arms wide and thrust his pelvis forward, "we have nothing to hide. What can I do for you?"

"I'm here about Jeron Nichols, a young man who disappeared over the weekend. The last place his friends saw him was here." He pulled out a picture of the man and handed it to Damon through the booth's window.

"He's a very handsome man," Damon said. "He'd be more than welcome here." His cock swelled and stood straighter. He handed the picture back to the policeman as his other hand mindlessly reached down and pulled up on his low-hanging, hairy balls. The pair swung back and forth, making his thick dick sway.

Ryan took the picture back and pulled out two more. "What about these men?" One was a yearbook picture of a husky football player and the other was a lean swimmer in a Speedo. Both men were handsome, young and model material.

Damon shook his head. "No. Sorry. Anything else I can do for you?" He handed the pictures back and stood up, again pushing his hips forward.

Ryan swallowed hard. "I would like to take a look around, but I don't have a warrant..."

"That shouldn't be a problem. I own Incubus Steams, and, just as I said, we have nothing to hide."

Ryan nodded, surprised at how easy it had been.

Damon reached over to the Peg-Board next to him and handed him an elastic ring with a plastic number on it and a key.

"What is this?"

"It's a locker key." Damon placed a towel on the counter and pushed it through the window.

"What's this?"

"If you want to come in and look around, you'll have to follow the rules, just like everyone else. No shoes, no shirt, no clothes. No nothing."

"I can't...I'm on duty."

"I can't make my customers feel uncomfortable while they're here. I don't allow any street clothes past the locker room." He pressed a button on the microphone next to the cash register. "Bill, can you come up to the front desk, please." His voice echoed through the building.

"I don't understand." Ryan turned the key over in his hand. The number 13 was carved into the plastic.

"Bill will cover the front desk for me, while I take you on a tour. Anything you want to see will be revealed." He picked up the towel on the chair he had vacated and wrapped it loosely around his narrow hips. He opened the door and stepped out into the lobby.

"I'm not sure..." Ryan started.

"I'm sure you have been to a Y or a health club, it's all the same thing, with a few different features and services offered. I'm sure you know what I mean." He winked at Ryan.

Ryan bit his lower lip. How did this young man know he was gay? He knew his arousal wasn't showing. Did his eyes reveal more about him than…? Did he spend too much time looking at his…?

Bill arrived with a towel wrapped around his waist and slipped into the vacated booth.

"Thanks, Bill. I'll be showing this officer around Incubus Steams. I'll be back once all of his questions have been answered."

"Take your time." Bill unwrapped his towel from his waist and set it on the chair. He bent forward showing a perfect, tight ass, smooth and white as cream. He sat down. His huge cock flopped over one leg. He adjusted himself and sat back as if he was sunning himself.

Damon motioned to the doorway that led to the locker room with an arrow painted on the wall. "After you," he said.

Ryan didn't move.

Damon reached over and took the key from his hand. "Thirteen, my lucky number." He walked through the doorway and along the red-carpeted hallway. Pictures of naked men in different poses covered the walls. A hollow, echoing ring could be heard at the end of the hallway, where the locker room was.

The floor was white tiled and wooden lockers lined the walls and made a maze in the room. A big, muscle-bound, black male showered in the biggest shower room ever. Thick foam flowed over his body as he washed between his cheeks. He looked over his shoulder and continued washing down his leg.

Damon walked over to number thirteen, inserted the key and opened the wooden door. He stood back to make room for Ryan to undress.

Ryan looked at him and then inside the locker. This wasn't a rusty health-club locker. This one held hangers and pull-out, rolling shelves for shoes and underwear. There was even a shelf with deodorant, toothbrush, toothpaste, comb, brush, razor, shaving cream, soap and cologne, everything you would need and not think to bring.

"We have everything you could ever want or need. Just ask, and you will receive." Damon's eyes glowed as he spoke.

Ryan didn't know what to do. He stood staring into the locker.

"Well," Damon said, "do you want the tour?"

Ryan hesitated for a second and slowly removed his jacket. He pulled out a hanger and hung it up, wrinkle free.

Damon watched his every move.

Ryan started and then stopped unbuttoning his shirt. "Are you sure this is necessary?"

"If you want to see beyond the locker room, it is." He never looked away. "Am I making you uncomfortable?"

Ryan shrugged and started to unbutton his shirt. He wouldn't give this kid the satisfaction of making him feel self-conscious. He worked out four times a week. He knew he had a great body. He just didn't want to be on display. Turning his back to the owner, he opened the shirt and placed it over another hanger. He pulled his T-shirt over his head as he kicked off his shoes. He bent over to pick them up.

Damon took careful notice of how the dress slacks hugged his muscular ass. The seam rode deep into his crease. *Boxers*, he thought, as Ryan unbuckled his belt and opened his fly. Blue-striped boxer-briefs covered his butt as he slipped out of the slacks, and electricity snapped over the hairy legs and fabric.

Ryan tossed his pants on a sliding shelf and pulled off his socks. He looked over his shoulder and saw Damon still stared at him. He took a deep breath and pushed his boxers down. They slid down to his ankles as he reached for his towel and wrapped it around his narrow waist, tucking one end in deep. He stepped out of his boxers and kicked them up to his hand.

"See, that wasn't too bad, now was it?" Damon walked around him and handed him the key. He noticed the way the detective's towel bulged in front of him. "Lock your stuff up, and then we can head in, unless you want to shower first?"

Ryan closed the locker and quickly locked it with the key. He stretched the elastic around his hairy wrist and let it snap closed. "I'm fine." His bare feet felt how warm the floor was.

"Everything is well heated and cleaned so no worries of infections or cold feet."

The black bodybuilder turned off the shower and walked to the entryway of the showers. He toweled the back of his head dry and showed his hairless body in all its wet, shining glory. His massive cock started to grow and swell as the men looked at him. He smiled at the attention.

"As you can see, this is a very friendly place," Damon stroked the bodybuilder's cock as they passed by. "If you went down the hallway to the left, you'd find private rooms. There is a loop of rooms to walk around and on busy nights there is a lot of bed-hopping going on."

"Is there anyone down there?" Ryan paused at the intersection.

"You are more than welcome to go down there, but I doubt you'll find anyone. It's still too early in the day."

"I would like to be the judge of that." Ryan started down the hallway and passed by room after empty room. They paused at one room where a naked man lay on his stomach, his bare ass centered in the open doorway.

"You're able to partake of anything you want to while you're here. You're my guest, free of charge. You can get a massage, a private room, whatever." He motioned to the naked man. "I'm sure he wouldn't mind a little attention." Damon entered the room, rubbed his hand over the fleshy mounds of the man's perfect ass. He spread his cheeks and slid a finger down his crack. "So tight, so hot, so available."

Ryan felt his cock swell underneath his towel, but he shook his head. "Tempting, but I'm sure there's more to see."

Damon slapped the man's butt. "He's not jumping at the first piece he sees, I respect that." He left the room. "Back to the tour."

The rest of the private rooms were empty, and Damon returned to the intersection. "Which way now? To the hot tubs, saunas, steam rooms, video rooms, massage tables, glory holes, bondage a-go-go?" Damon looked into his eyes. "You want to see them all, don't you? Follow me."

They went to the hot tubs, which bubbled with no one inside; a row of rooms that looked like changing rooms in a clothing store lined one wall. "Glory, glory, hole-alleluia." Damon pushed the swinging doors open. "There are holes between the booths and," he motioned to walk around the side, "a wall of wieners over here." A few dicks poked out of holes and slipped back inside, like gophers at the zoo.

On the other side of the wall, a round stage dominated the center of the room, and the stage's floor glowed. Cameras and video monitors were everywhere in the room. Not an inch of the wall space was empty.

Ryan watched as they walked to the stage. Damon dropped his towel and jumped on top. All the video monitors suddenly showed every angle of his body. The light in the floor intensified and the cameras missed nothing. Even a camera from beneath the stage showed his ass and hairy balls in all their beauty.

"Did you ever want to be on TV?"

Ryan handed the towel up and waited.

Damon ignored it. "All our recordings are saved for six months, in case anything happens that we need to go back and review."

"I would like to see Friday, Saturday, and Sunday night's tapes."

"That can be arranged. Would you like to view them here? Or in my office?"

"Your office would be easier."

"Anything else you'd like to see?" Damon stepped on a button, and a dildo rose out of the floor like a microphone at an award show. There was a camera in the tip, and as it rose, Damon's balls and tight ass came into a sharp view. A line of black hair circled his pink opening. On one video monitor, his tender bud grew and grew in size. A sheen of lube flowed over the lens as it got closer to his hole.

Damon leaned forward, using the monitors to guide himself into the perfect position on stage. He lowered himself slightly over the ascending phallus, and he impaled himself on it. Images from every angle flooded the screens, even a view from deep inside Damon. His foot worked the pole that rose and fell from the stage. He rode the rod, moaning as he did.

Ryan tied his towel tighter as it threatened to slip off. He adjusted his cock as it doubled in size.

"You can join me onstage. There is another internal cam." He rocked his hips and swayed back and forth.

A naked man emerged from one of the glory-hole booths. Working his raging hard-on, he took a spot next to the stage and stared up at Damon as he jacked off. He waved Ryan over.

Music started and laser lights swirled around, but Ryan stepped back into the shadows to watch. A camera zoomed in on Damon's cock and showed a pearl of precum pooling at the tip. The laser light hit it, making it glow an iridescent pink then purple. Streaks of electricity sparked over his tan skin, and his eyes glowed even brighter.

The man jacked his dick harder and harder. His balls rose, and he arched his back as an arc of semen sprayed across the stage. A camera caught his action and replayed it from several different angles, over and over in a loop, making it look like a Niagara Falls of orgasms.

Ryan mused that football games and convenience stores should have as good camera work as security. He rubbed his erection. Savoring the sensation, but not willing to release his load.

Damon groaned and shot his load across the stage at the naked man. He pumped out his cum and milked out a small pool on the floor. His bare foot stepped on the button, and the dildo cam retracted from his ass and descended into the floor. The beautiful image of his ass disappeared too.

The naked man reached onto the stage and scooped up Damon's seed and rubbed it over his lips and into his mouth. He fingered his face as he continued to work his cock.

Damon walked to him at the edge of the stage, knelt down and let him clean his dick and suck out the last few drops of cum. He stood, ruffled the man's hair and jumped down from the stage.

The man grabbed and slapped Damon's ass as he headed over to Ryan.

Damon turned and said, "I'll find you later, we can finish what you started..." and he winked and thrust his ass out to him. As he neared Ryan, he wrapped his towel around his hips. "I have to make the customers happy, give them what they want and make them beg for more. You'll see..."

Ryan worried at that last comment, but followed him out of the video area. A hallway arrow read SAUNA AND STEAM⇨.

"I doubt this is what you came for. I bet you want to see the real deal." The men walked side by side down the darkened hallway.

"How did you come up with the name Incubus Steams?" Ryan broke the silence and tried to steer the tour back to the information he needed and not sex. He hoped that would help calm his arousal.

Damon smiled. "I used Incubus for the sexual content of this place pure and simple. I wanted to use Dreams, but I felt that Steam told more about the business. It rhymed with dreams so I figured I could use it as a double entendre and make this place mysterious, sexy and a little scary. Do you like to be scared, Ryan?" His voice was soft and smooth, caressing with each syllable.

Ryan nodded before he could stop himself.

An open door showed a naked man lying on his back with two men, one on each side, massaging every inch of him. Oil flowed over his body and off the table. The masseurs' arms glistened above the elbow. One man worked the massive cock as the other worked between his buttcheeks.

"There is always time for a four-hand massage..."

Ryan inhaled deeply: the scent of man, sex and coconuts filled the room. "I'm good."

"That you are," Damon licked his lips as he looked down at Ryan's damp towel. "I think you're gonna need a new towel, soon."

"I'm fine."

"That you are..." Damon opened a cabinet on the wall and pulled out a new fresh towel and handed it to him. "If you need..."

The carpeting ended and the floor turned into heated tile. A wooden door with a window radiated heat as they neared.

SAUNA was engraved into a sign on the door.

Damon pulled the wooden handle open and motioned for Ryan to enter. A wall of humid heat slammed into them. "Hurry, so we don't let the heat out." He pushed Ryan inside and followed close behind and slammed the door.

Two men rolled on the bottom step in each other's arms, kissing and licking each other's face as their hands caressed all over.

A man on the top bench flung a ladle full of water onto the hot stones and steam formed immediately as the water evaporated instantly. The air in the room expanded with enough strength to force open the door.

Sweat broke out over Ryan's body and ran down, instantly soaking his towel.

"Told you," Damon said. He sat down on a middle bench and motioned for Ryan to join him.

Ryan reluctantly sat down, towel still tightly wrapped around his hips.

Damon spread his legs. The scent of sweat, semen and something else rose from his body and mixed with the humidity. He ran his finger up Ryan's leg and pushed the towel up and open.

Ryan clamped his hand down and stopped him.

"I've seen it already."

Ryan looked nervously around the room.

Damon smiled. "Oh, I get it. Follow me." He wrapped his towel around his waist and pulled Ryan out of the sauna. "This way." He pointed to the writing on the wall: STEAM ROOM.

They turned the corner and found a glass door with a metal frame. Damon picked up a sign and hooked it over the metal bar on the steam room's door: CLOSED FOR CLEANING. "This will give us the privacy you want."

Ryan entered the steam room: a thick mist filled the tiled room, drops of water dripping from the ceiling as more steam billowed from the metal pipes. Eucalyptus hung in the humidity and cleared his sinus passages. The heat soaked into his body and made his limbs feel heavy. His new towel drooped and clung to his skin, the thin white cotton almost see-through.

Damon sat on the wooden bench and made room for Ryan.

Ryan sat down next to him and inhaled deeply. The moist heat flowed over his body as if in a tropical jungle.

Damon moved closer and guided Ryan's body to lie down on the bench. He lifted his hairy legs up and cradled his feet in his lap. He massaged his feet and ran his thumbs up the arch of each foot and sent shivers across his body.

Ryan felt his body start to relax for the first time since he had entered Incubus Steams. His towel grew heavy over his waist, and slowly he relaxed his hold.

Damon gently opened the towel and allowed Ryan to finally be free. He watched as Ryan's cock flipped up and lay over his abdomen. Damon rubbed up his legs and thumbed along his inseam.

Ryan's hairy balls rose as something fluttered over them. His cock jerked, rocking up and down, and precum oozed out of his tip. The moist heat relaxed him. He stroked his penis once to adjust himself and then felt the precum flow out of him and fill his belly button.

"Now, you get it," Damon cooed. "Let your body go, close your eyes, breathe deeply, sleep..."

Ryan's eyelids grew heavy, and he exhaled deeply, drifting, floating...

Damon rose and straddled his hips. He reached back and pulled Ryan's cock up and sat on it. His butt was still lubed from the dildo cam on stage.

Ryan's dick entered him easily. He reached up and ran his hands over his torso and down to his hips. His fingers curled around his waist and pulled Damon's pelvis down on his dick. He thrust up with his hips and enjoyed the pulsating muscle as it swallowed his cock.

Damon combed his fingers across Ryan's hairy chest. His hand slipped easily with the sweat and humidity. He increased his speed as he rode the thick cock drilling his ass. With one hand he jacked himself as he bounced. Instead of relaxing, his butt sphincter tightened and increased the stimulation on Ryan's dick.

Faster and faster, their rate increased. Ryan pulled down harder and harder on Damon's hips, driving deeper inside. The pleasure grew and grew.

Damon's ass bore down on his dick, and Ryan couldn't last any longer. His cock exploded again and again with each thrust. White-hot cream flowed out of him and filled Damon.

As the last drop shot into him, Damon bounded off of Ryan and spread his legs. He oiled his dick and slammed it into Ryan's ass.

Ryan gasped as the sensory overload took his body. He arched his back and allowed easier access to his butt. He grabbed onto the bench and lifted his legs up and opened them wider to allow for full penetration.

Damon's hips pushed into him, and his thick cock swelled, doubling in girth. His body heat increased also.

Ryan opened his eyes and watched as Damon started to glow; his whole body swelled and pulsated with an unearthly light. The feeling was amazing, and his cop mind didn't care what happened next; he felt his body warm, then heat up. Pressure built inside him, but the pleasure was too good, he wanted more and more.

Damon drilled into him with all his might; he could feel the climax simmering in his balls turn into a full rapid boil. Heat, cum and light shot out of him and into Ryan.

Ryan screamed in the most intense pleasure of his life.

Damon pumped into him one more time, emptying his balls, and watched as Ryan's body exploded in a burst of steam, semen and blood.

An outline of Ryan remained on the wooden bench, but the rest of him was splattered everywhere. Damon licked the back of his hand and wiped the goo from his eyes. "Wow, that was a hot one." He stood on unsteady legs and skated over to the corner, where a hose hung on the wall. He turned on the faucet and let the cool water wash over his body.

Once he was clean, he looked around the steam room. "Why no, Officer Ryan, I have no idea where all the handsome young men have disappeared to." He looked at the gooey mess on the walls, the floor and the ceiling. He grabbed the hose and started to wash everything down the drain. "Do you?"

Officer Ryan awoke and sat up with a gasp as the cold water splashed over his sweaty body.

"You don't mind if I rinse you off? Do you?" Damon asked, innocently.

The water washed the blobs of semen off him and cooled his feverish flesh.

"Sometimes bad boys need to disappear, and good ones..." Damon continued to hose him off. "All clean."

"Thanks," Ryan stood and grabbed for his towel to dry off. "I need to go, and get back to work."

"You're welcome back anytime, and I hope you find those missing boys. The good turn up and the bad ones..."

"I will, just give me time."

"You can have all the time you need." Damon kissed him, knowing he was a good one, and he'd stay.

STEAM PUNK

Eric Del Carlo

Gay bathhouses offer anonymity, and that's why they're so popular. You don't even have to talk to anyone. You can just enjoy the bodies of men.

But a bathhouse, I've always found, is also a place of raw honesty. You are literally exposed, with nothing to hide behind except those skimpy white towels that most of the men quickly toss aside. Every inch of you will be inspected by ravenous eyes as you move from pool to steam-filled room.

The place I went to was in an old industrial building in the city's warehouse district. You wouldn't know it was a business just by looking at the grimy, stony exterior. But inside it was always jumping, every night. It was almost like a maze, with tiled passageways branching off every which way.

I paid the nameless guy at the desk and went to dump my clothes in a locker. The bathhouse staff kept a very low profile. Some men got nervous whenever anyone official was around. I could tell which ones had wives and felt sorry for them. I'd never had to lead a double life, for which I was grateful. I had been sexually active with men for the twenty years of my adulthood and had never had to apologize or lie to anybody.

My flesh was already prickling, that first low-level arousal that comes even before your cock starts to stir, when there is only anticipation. I'd been looking forward to this all day. I draped my white towel over a shoulder and padded barefoot out into the maze. At six five and with a job that kept me physically fit, I knew I cut an impressive figure. But I wasn't one of those gym-rat types who only wanted to fuck around with mirror images of themselves. I liked all kinds of men, and the bathhouse, as always, had lots of masculine possibilities on display tonight.

I passed by the main pool, where a couple dozen men were checking each other out. Some of these guys, I knew, would make a grab for the first man they saw. I wasn't that indiscriminate anymore. I needed to be genuinely attracted to a man, even an anonymous one, if I was going to screw around with him. Otherwise I could just stay home and jerk off.

I headed down a corridor. The bathhouse sprawled, and even though I knew the layout, I always felt like I could get lost here. That was part of the fun, like wandering through a wonderland of steam and male lust.

Along the way there were sauna rooms and smaller jet-pools. Guys were gathered there too. And some were doing more than just *gathering*. In one whirling pool two men grappled in the water, lips pressed together in warm kisses, hands pulling at hard cocks. A little crowd of eager onlookers sat along the edge, enjoying the show.

Farther along, a door was ajar. I looked into one of the steam rooms. Plumes of hot vapor made it look ghostly inside, but I spotted the guy on his hands and knees on the damp floorboards who was getting his ass eaten out by a burly dude with long, slick-wet blond hair that was plastered across his broad shoulders.

Grinning, I kept heading along the rounded tunnel-like corridor. Suddenly, I heard a voice echoing off the tiles: "I told you, get the fuck away from me!"

It tripped some instinct in me, and I found myself hurrying to the corner, adrenaline starting to pump. It sounded like somebody in trouble, but when I came around the turn, I stopped short. And gaped. And caught myself just before I erupted into laughter.

The sight was so absurd. There in the middle of the corridor was a skinny, tattooed kid, pale with boot-polish black hair in a limp Mohawk. He crouched facing away from me, buck naked, and he was swinging a wet towel over his head, whipping it at a fat troll of a guy with bad skin and a leering grin. Naturally, there were no staff members on hand.

"You ain't layin' a paw on me, motherfucker, so back off!" the punk-type kid yelled.

It was pretty easy to figure out what had happened. I recognized the troll. He had boundary issues, and had been a problem before. He looked to be about twice the body mass of the stick-thin punk.

Again, I let instinct dictate my move. Without another second of hesitation, I went past the kid and blocked the corridor. "You want to keep going with this, I'll be happy to call the cops," I said to the plump predator, even though it was obvious I wasn't carrying a phone. "No means no, asshole."

He gave me an indignant look, but quickly retreated. I turned around.

The punk glared at me. He had thin, dark-red lips, and his eyes were like extinguished coals. He wanted everyone to know what a tough piece of work he was. He said, "You think I'm gonna be grateful to you now? Think you're gonna get a blow job out of this, old man? Well, you can fuckin' forget it."

He gave his towel another menacing swing. He was muscle and bone, and nothing else: a lean, lovely body, marked by at least six tattoos. He couldn't be a day over twenty.

"Fucking forget about it I will," I said amiably, smiling. Maybe I hadn't expected gratitude, but I sure didn't need this adolescent bullshit. I turned and sauntered away.

Later I heard him padding along behind me. I gave him a glance. He had the damp towel around his middle, while mine was still draped casually over my shoulder.

"You want something?" I asked.

He looked at the floor. "I'm sorry I called you *old man*."

I laughed. "Compared to you I am so no worries. What else do you want?" Because he had to be following me for a reason.

"I..." He traced a square of tile with his big toe, still looking down. "I've never been here before. I, um, don't really know how it's s'posed to work." He raised his head. Heat had flowed into his eyes. "Can you show me?"

It was like that injection of adrenaline from a minute ago. My blood raced, and gooseflesh stood out on my arms. "Sure," I said, voice suddenly hoarse. "Let's go in here." I led him into a small nearby sauna room.

I was glad to find it empty. Not that I had a problem with anyone looking at me, but this kid was new to the scene, like he'd said. For all I knew, this was his first gay adventure.

The space was maybe twelve feet long, with a low ceiling. A wooden platform was against one wall. The air was thick with a hot dampness. I had worked hard all day, and that heat felt good. Immediately, sweat started coursing out of me, rolling down my chest. I tossed down my towel and sat on the bench.

The punk stood there, looking around. I wondered if he lived on the streets. No, I decided. Despite his thinness, he didn't look malnourished. He really was a sleek little treat.

"My name's Dale," I said. "And by telling you that, I'm breaking an unspoken rule of the bathhouse. The guys who come here like to keep it anonymous."

"I'm Curt."

"Nice to meet you, Curt. Sit down if you want. The steam feels good." I leaned back, luxuriating in the heat as it got down into my sore muscles.

He kept the towel on as he sat, but I saw him looking at my naked body. I was willing myself not to get a hard-on, despite how sexy I found Curt. I didn't want to spook him, not after he'd had that bad encounter with the troll.

After a quiet minute he said, "I like how you look." His dark eyes flashed away, and I actually saw a blush on his cheek.

It was endearing as hell. "I like how you look too. You're beautiful, Curt." My voice shook a little as I added, "I'd like to see all of you again."

He hesitated, but just for a second. Then he stood and peeled off the towel. I sat up, drinking in his body, studying him shamelessly now. His cock was rising from a nest of dark wiry curls, and that was like a signal to me. My thick cockhead rolled up my bare sweaty thigh. I watched him watching me.

"I never done this before!" he blurted. His shallow chest was rising and falling. I could see each one of his ribs. "I mean, I'm no virgin. I messed around with guys before, but it's always been with some ugly shithead or somebody who just wants to get himself off and leaves me hanging—"

I was surprised to see tears spring into his eyes. I stood and stepped toward him, moved. I folded him into my arms. His narrow body felt good against mine, but this contact was more than sexual. Curt had a rough time of it—bad sex partners, unlucky situations.

"It's okay," I told him, stroking his damp un-gelled Mohawk. His face was nuzzled against my neck, his arms holding me tight. I felt his still-hardening cock against my leg.

His lips brushed my throat as the steam continued to rise all around us. "I figured if I came to a place like this," I heard him murmur, "maybe I'd find somebody, who, y'know..."

I could have told him he *had* found someone that would treat him right, but words were cheap.

Slipping a knuckle under his chin to gently tilt back his head, I bent to press my lips against his. I felt his body stiffen. He returned my kiss. I didn't rush it; I was too busy savoring.

Our kisses deepened, at which point he boldly thrust his tongue into my mouth. It was luscious. His fingers dug into my back. His cock surged into full hardness. He was rubbing against my leg. I was practically licking his tonsils as I caressed his back with my other hand, tracing his spine down to the taut halves of his ass.

Curt moaned into my mouth. He pushed against me but not to shove me away. Together we stumbled toward the broad wood bench, still kissing crazily. He had a wiry strength to him, with enough muscle in that slim body to force me down onto the platform. It occurred to me how lucky that bad-skinned troll from before was. If he'd tried anything serious, Curt probably would have put out his lights.

I was lying back now, the damp wood warm underneath me. Sweat streamed into my eyes. Curt, with a flushed face, collapsed on top of me. I opened my arms as he laid his hard, lithe body on mine. We kissed again. He writhed, grinding his cock against mine, which sent pleasure through my slick body. I groped his flexing ass again, pressing a finger against his asshole.

A few strands of his dyed black Mohawk had fallen over his eyes. Beads of sweat dripped down the shaved sides of his skull. Both his ears were pierced with lots of studs. As he continued to wriggle his slippery body on top of mine, I realized one of his nipples was pierced.

I wondered about the sex he'd had with those other guys; if there'd been time for niceties like this. Nobody had ever come close to *making love* to Curt, I felt sure.

He sucked my nipples, grinning between licks. Even as my excitement rose and my back arched under me, I kept an eye on his sweet young face. Bliss washed over his features. He caught me with his teeth, but he was gentle about it, following instincts he probably didn't know he had. Then he traded off to my left nip.

"I gotta have your cock in my mouth!" he said.

I grinned. "Yeah. Suck it. Please." My heart was thudding in my chest.

I continued to watch him as he kissed and nibbled his way down my body. My cock was straining, desperate for the touch of his moist lips. He settled between my legs, his hard bony shoulders pressing apart my thighs. His shapely ass pointed up in the air as he lowered his mouth.

Stray hairs tickled my belly as his fingers took hold of my shaft at its thick base. His other hand closed lightly around my balls. Resting on his elbows, he gave my cockhead a tentative lick. *Maybe he won't like it*, I thought. *Maybe this will remind him of bad past experiences*. But I was being silly. Curt's tongue went swirling wildly over my fat plum, and my whole body squirmed with pleasure.

My nipples ached from the thorough sucking he'd given them. My balls stirred in his delicate grip. I was mesmerized by the sight of Curt's lips around the head of my cock, his mouth dropping inch by inch down my veined piece. He swallowed me to my balls. My head thumped back down on the bench. My eyes were closed to the intense sexual joy.

His tongue worked me over. When his head rose, I cried out loud when he dropped his mouth again. He maintained a perfect suction as he started a bobbing rhythm on me. Whatever else he'd taken away from his previous sexual escapades, he'd sure learned how to suck a cock!

Red flashes were going off on the backs of my eyelids. Steam coated me, and sweat continued to roll off my body. The heat of the sauna was nothing compared to the seething, living warmth of Curt's talented mouth. Carnal energy radiated outward from my cock, spreading to every part of me. My limbs tingled. My toes bunched. I was thrusting up with every downward plunge he made. My hips were trying to lift up from the platform. Curt kept a grip on me with his hands and mouth.

I let loose a wail. My hands flailed at my sides. Curt's speed increased. Finally I had to see his beautiful face, even as my orgasm started to overtake me.

I lifted my head, just as my balls tightened and my hot, heavy juice started to fly. Curt, who could feel it on its way, wrenched his mouth off me. My cum shot over his shoulder, a few pearly flecks dotting the shaved side of his head. He grabbed my shaft and started pumping furiously. Pleasure ripped through my body.

Curt was grinning again, watching the white globs land. He jerked me through my last few quivering spasms, then let go of my softening cock. I was panting, barely able to get a breath, but I felt wonderful. It had been a *cum* to remember. Even the afterglow felt great.

I wiped my damp face with a damp palm, unsure where I'd tossed my towel. But when I looked at Curt again, he'd stopped grinning. In fact, he'd shrunk away from me on the bench, an uncertain look on his face.

Uneasiness grabbed me, but then I realized. He was afraid I was going to ditch him now that I'd gotten off. I silently cursed the assholes who'd been so uncaring with him. I sat up and reached out my hand.

"Come here," I said.

He gave me his hand, and I pulled him to me, closing my arms over him again. I smelled my cum on him. I kissed his temple, feeling a vein beating there.

"That was fantastic," I murmured. "Now let me do the same for you."

He sat up on the wood bench, feet planted on the ground and legs spread. I knelt on the floor, the soggy boards giving a little under my knees. Curt's cock reared up before me, the crown swollen, the shaft veiny. He had a tattoo on either hip, I saw. One was an Oriental character, the other a flaming skull. I took hold of his meat, feeling his pulse beat urgently. I had a last look up through the steam, seeing him gazing down at me, mouth open and eyes wide. He wanted it so bad.

I gave it to him.

When I licked his cockhead with my tongue, his knees clamped my shoulders. I felt the coiled strength of him. I loved the texture of his knob and rolled my lips over it until he let out a needy groan. I plunged down his staff, taking him all the way in a single swallow.

I buried my nose in his damp, dark curls, inhaling his scent. I took his cock down my throat, holding it there. My tongue continued to strum his shaft. I lifted my head, keeping my lips sealed around him, squeezing him. I knew my talents as a cocksucker, and I wanted to share everything I had with Curt.

As I started bobbing up and down on him, his strong narrow

body jerked. His ass fidgeted on the wood, and his bony knees gripped my shoulders harder, like a vise. He moaned louder. I kept up a deliberate speed, wanting him to enjoy the experience.

Pretty soon he let me know how much he was liking it: "That's so fuckin' good! I can't believe how good you suck!"

The corners of my stretched-out mouth turned up in a secret smile as I continued to blow him. But he deserved the full benefit of the experience. I wriggled my free hand beneath his sweat-slick ass, finding his hole and slipping a fingertip up into him. He just about shrieked with pleasure. His hands were suddenly raking through my hair. His hips rose. He was face-fucking me.

I probed his ass deeper, wiggling my finger up to the knuckle. I felt his sweet, tight passage clamping around my digit. He pulled harder at my hair. He was shouting more things now, but I couldn't hear. Blood roared in my ears. I sucked him faster, mouth slurping, everything a blur of flesh and steam.

My finger was all the way up into him when I felt his cock start to spasm. Reluctantly I pulled my mouth off him as he began to shoot. Hot droplets spattered my shoulder, and I smelled the beautiful salty tang. His ass muscles clenched as spurt after spurt jerked from his cock.

He let go of my hair. I sat back on my haunches, looking up at him. He lay back limp and spent, a look of satisfaction on his pale face. He knew what it was all about, I thought, and I was happy for him. I was glad no one had interrupted us. That got me thinking that it might be nice to see Curt outside the bathhouse, someplace private. But that could wait.

Smiling, he reached down for me, and I climbed up to nestle with him again, my new steamy punk lover.

RAF'S JOURNEY

Rafaelito V. Sy

His name was Hank Harney; this Raf couldn't forget. Five years had passed since they had met for the one and only time, and still Raf remembered Hank Harney's name and face, continued to relish in his thoughts Hank's smell and taste. From the moment Hank said his first and last names, the alliteration stuck with Raf—as did the pun of the surname *Harney* with the word *horny*.

"Don't even start," Hank said, smiling into Raf's eyes. He spoke with a voice that was part reproachful, part enticing whisper.

Raf chuckled. "So I'm not the first to call you Hank Horny," he said.

"I've had it all my life."

"And now you're at the age where you feel you need to live up to your alternate name."

"Now's as good a time as ever. And the perfect place."

The time was 2:00 a.m., the hour that guys trickle out of

bars and check into a bathhouse for another chance at man-to-man bonding. The place was the West Side Club on 27 West 20th Street in the heart of Chelsea, less than a stone's throw away from the Limelight. That was where Raf had come from: the Limelight.

How ironic that a cathedral should be converted into a nightclub, Raf always thought whenever he walked past the Limelight's portals.

The irony didn't bother him. It delighted him. That a bathhouse should be situated a couple of yards away dispelled much of what he had been preached to believe about his true nature. Raf had left the Philippines a decade earlier to attend college in the United States for exactly this reason—the freedom to express his love the way he had been born to love. No damnation in that.

Of every metropolis in America, New York represented salvation. New York was not any city. It was the city where *Boys in the Band* had been filmed and where the image of a bronzed man in Calvin Klein underwear once loomed over Times Square. In New York, Raf found the community he had longed for and he found many beautiful men. But he had not found love. Not yet. College had been four years of furtive glances, of masturbating under the sheets to fantasies of jocks he dared not approach. There was the rugby player with a sturdy voice and dark hair that always looked windswept, who worked at a deli and delivered Raf his cheesesteak sub every midnight; the captain of the crew team, dimple on his chin, bulging biceps peppered with red freckles, who sat quietly at the back of psychology class, doodling in his notebook. There was the whole fucking football team.

I'm too thin, Raf thought during those college years. *I'm clumsy with a ball. I don't slap high fives.*

He dared not approach the objects of his desire, yet he never forgot why he had decided on America as his new home. Raf was eighteen when he had arrived, the ripe age for growth. He eventually took to wearing button-down shirts that flattered his naturally broad shoulders rather than shirts that seemed a size too large, and he replaced his penny loafers with lumberjack boots. He learned how to read the health chart on fast-food boxes and developed a routine of going to the gym two days a week. Two days a week increased to three and then four. His five-seven, 135-pound frame added 15 pounds of muscles by graduation. His watch became too small to fit on his wrist.

The changes Raf witnessed in the mirror resulted in other transformations. He walked with his back straight rather than stooped in uncertainty. His stride was fast and sure rather than timidly slow. And when interviewing for jobs as a photographer, he impressed with the daringness of his street shots as much as he did with the strength of his handshake. New York was no longer a labyrinth in which he was a child lost amid a swirl of people too focused on their destination to lend a helping hand. At last, Raf knew where he was going. Sleepless nights at the Roxy and the Limelight, shirtless, his torso glistening in sweat under pulsating strobe lights; a truck parked along a pavement littered with broken beer bottles, where he dropped to his knees and sucked off an Italian bodybuilder while finger-fucking the stranger's ass; dark corners in dark places, on his back, bent over, against a wall, swallowing penises and tongues in both his orifices—Raf was going forward. Full speed ahead.

Raf's journey led to Hank Harney. Hank was twenty-seven years old with a swimmer's sculpted body. His eyes were nutmeg brown. His short hair was the hue of honey and sun. Raf was twenty-nine. Though Raf still had a boyish air about him (his smile was the one thing that refused to age), he now possessed a man's powerful chest and set of thighs. Hank was walking down the hallway lined with opened doors, smiling at each guy standing at the threshold of his room, but stopping at none. A mirror behind Hank revealed his asscrack peeking out from above the towel wrapped around his waist. That was what Raf was focused on, the man's asscrack. Raf had just stepped out of his own room at the end of the hallway toward which Hank was headed. He expected nothing from Hank; no eye contact occurred between them. So he looked past Hank, at the reflection of Hank's backside in the distance diminishing in size as Hank neared him. He imagined the towel falling, his fingers sliding down Hank's ass, spreading Hank's buttcheeks and tickling his anus, stretching Hank's asshole open and sliding a finger in. He imagined Hank groaning and hugging him for support as Hank tightened his sphincter around the finger. He imagined how Hank would kiss him, fondle his nipples, work a hand from his cock to his balls then to his butthole and whisper, "Man, let's fuck."

Raf imagined.

Hank stopped. He smiled. His smile emanated daylight, all teeth and soft furrows at the corners of his eyes. Raf looked to either side of him to see who else might have been present to be the rightful recipient of that smile, but there was no mistake; it was directed at him.

"Are you okay?" Hank asked with a chuckle.

"Yeah," Raf said. "You've taken me by surprise, that's all."

"I'm sorry."

"Oh, no. It's a nice surprise. It's..."

Hank moved closer, ran the back of his hand down Raf's chest to the navel, and grabbed Raf's towel.

"It's great," said Raf.

"Like the way you feel."

Raf took Hank by the hand and into his room then slammed the door shut. Their towels fell off. Raf grabbed Hank's face and kissed him, slowly, sliding his tongue into Hank's mouth, probing the insides. Hank responded by sucking on Raf's tongue. Their hard penises pressed against their navels. Music was playing on the loudspeaker in the hallway—heavy bass, violin swirls—but the one sound that dominated Raf's being was Hank's hungry breathing. His breath warmed Raf's face, as if Hank were trying to inhale Raf, swallow Raf into the hotness of his mouth.

The two remained standing. They caressed each other's back and buttock. The room was large enough only for a cot and two naked bodies. A mirror lined the wall across from the cot. Over Hank's shoulder, Raf glimpsed the reflection of the ass that he had been fantasizing about a mere few seconds earlier.

Unbelievable that life can change in the blink of an eye.

Raf abruptly pulled himself away from Hank, though he kept their hands clasped together.

Hank gave a startled look. "Anything the matter?" he asked.

"I want to look at you for a moment to see that this is really happening," Raf said.

Hank's buttcheeks were baby smooth and fair, while his five-ten body was beach bronzed. Yet it was winter. The first offering of snow was piling on the city streets and naked before Raf was a guy who seemed to have just strutted off a Caribbean cruise. And he was hot to the touch.

"You're literally smoldering," Raf said.

"The steam room."

Hank's prick was slim and reached his belly button. A drop of precum glistened at the tip of his mushroom head and a tuft of blond pubic hair was shaved into an inverted triangle. That was the way Raf liked his man's cock the most—wet with semen to be used as lube; lean and lengthy so that he could feel it slide against his inner butt walls, penetrate his second sphincter.

"Now let me look at you," Hank said.

Raf let go of Hank's hands and slightly raised his arms sideways in offering himself for appraisal. Raf's body was an even tone of brown. His pecks were round. Muscles and power veined his arms. When he turned his backside to Hank, he heard Hank gush, "Oh, man. Fuck, yeah." He felt Hank's hand on his butt. Hank's touch was gentle, loving. A finger slid against Raf's ass-slit. This elicited a groan from both the admirer and the admired.

With one swift motion, Hank swung Raf around so that the two were face-to-face once more. They fell onto the cot, Hank on top of Raf. Raf raised his arms above his head. Hank clamped Raf's wrists down. They continued to kiss, more forcefully now, greedily. If there was anything that Hank taught Raf at that moment it was the erotic possibility of the chin, the cheekbone, the neck, for it wasn't only Raf's tongue Hank sucked on. Hank made love to Raf's entire face.

"Look at you," Hank said. "Look at you."

Raf turned to his right and peered at his reflection in the mirror. Hank turned to where Raf directed his gaze. In the mirror their eyes met.

"You're beautiful," Hank said.

"You make me beautiful," said Raf.

In college, Hank's words were words Raf associated with others, never with himself. When his body started to change, compliments started coming. Nevertheless, the compliments were not entirely believable. Although they did their share in boosting his confidence, he forgot them as quickly as they had been uttered because those who had uttered them never stayed. And so Raf found himself in a cycle of searching for more—more men, more praise, more love. Now here was Hank Harney.

How real was this?

Hank raised Raf's legs and sucked on Raf's butthole. Raf smiled. It seemed Hank was reading his mind: Raf would take as much as he could of this man Hank Harney to keep with him for the rest of his life.

"Open up for me," Hank said.

Raf pushed out his rectum. "How does it taste?" he asked.

"Like jock skank."

"Exactly, homobitch."

Hank got out from in between Raf's legs. He straddled Raf's chest, grabbed Raf by the hair and rammed his jizz-dripping penis into Raf's mouth. Hank was deep throat-fucking so ferociously that Raf was gagging. Tears welled in Raf's eyes. He released Hank's cock for a moment of air. Before he had a chance to fully catch his breath, the top shoved the bottom's face up his manhole.

"Breathe my juicy asshole," Hank said. "Asphyxiate on that, you gorgeous piece of butt meat."

Raf obeyed. He did more than obey. He smothered Hank's asshole with his entire face. Hank smelled of man sweat and coconut oil. He tasted of cum and sleaze.

Once more, Hank was on top of Raf. Raf wrapped his legs around Hank's back. The tip of Hank's cock poked Raf's twitching hole and slid inside. Hank moaned. Raf moaned. Every thrust increased in momentum. Every thrust generated yet another moan. And their moans were in unison. In the dim light, Hank's dark eyes grew bright. Sweat trickled down his forehead, dripped onto Raf's face. Raf sucked on Hank's chin, sucked on his nose, his cheekbones and earlobes, did everything Hank had just taught him.

"Harder," Raf said. His legs were no longer around Hank but were flailing in the air. "Fuck me the hardest that you've ever fucked in your gorgeous stud-dude butt-fucking life."

Hank opened his mouth. He looked delirious. He looked like he was about to scream but no sound came out. And then he yelled. Sperm gushed out of him. Raf felt Hank's orgasm as an explosion in his bowels. Hank's cum was spewing out like water from a fire hose, spilling out of Raf's slut-hole, dripping down his asscrack and forming a puddle on the sheets.

Hank collapsed on top of Raf, ran his fingers through Raf's hair. He was tender again, loving again. He kept his manhood inside Raf. Raf could still feel Hank's cock pulsating, releasing the last drops of semen. The fucker refused to let go until he pumped up every muscle in Raf's body with his fluids.

"What's your name?" Raf asked.

Hank laughed. He looked into Raf's eyes and he blinked flirtatiously. His eyes were still bright. "Hank," he said.

"I'm Raf. Raf Sanchez. Your last name?"

"Harney."

"Hank Harney. Or Hank Horny."

"Don't even start," Hank said with a blush.

They needed more of each other, so Hank invited Raf back to his hotel. Hank was in town for a graphic design conference. He lived in Los Angeles and had extended his stay to include a weekend of debauchery.

"You're the big-bang ending of my visit," he told Raf.

Hank was neat. No clothes were strewn on the bed. No shoes and towels were scattered on the floor. An armoire was open to reveal shirts neatly folded in a suitcase. A red baseball cap atop a UCLA sweatshirt was on the dresser table. Both men unlaced their boots and removed their socks, placed their coats and jeans on an armchair. They flung off their underwear. Naked, Hank led Raf to the bathroom, where he turned on the shower over the tub.

Lights reflected off a marble countertop, cream tiles and walls. The tone of their bodies was more lustrous in the light. Hank's eyes didn't lose their sheen. They were so dark, yet vibrant as varnished mahogany. Raf's buzz cut showed skin. His eyes were as black as his hair. Every which way he turned, his eyes radiated a glow in the mirror.

Was Raf in the military? Was he a gymnast? A wrestler?

These were questions guys sometimes asked Raf. Their curiosity allowed him to act upon any fantasy he wanted. But tonight with Hank, he was none of these. He was just...Raf.

As they stepped into the bathtub, Raf wondered about the forces of the universe that had brought him to this particular man of all the men at the West Side Club. Of all the men available to Hank, why had he chosen Raf?

Under the sprinkling water, they lathered each other's body with soap. Hank faced Raf then propped one leg on the rim of the tub. Raf slid his hand across Hank's butthole, tickled the asslips with his fingers.

"That feels really good," Hank said, tilting his head back and caressing his hair, squirting water out of his mouth. He brought one hand to Raf's erect dick and stroked.

"Why me?" Raf asked. "Of all the guys there?"

Hank kept on stroking. He gazed into Raf's eyes. "I was wondering the same thing about you," he said. "Why me?"

"We just gravitated to each other, I guess. Like steel to magnet."

"Chemistry."

"Is chemistry that palpable in the midst of a crowd? From across a hallway? A club?"

"God, yes," Hank said.

Shower water continued to trickle on them. The water was warm, soothing. Now that a piece of Hank was inside Raf, they could never be separate. Even though they would say good-bye at sunrise, Hank was a part of Raf for the rest of his life. Whatever men Raf had had before this ceased to exist. Whatever men he would have in the future didn't matter. The only reality Raf knew was Hank.

Five years had passed since they met for that one and only time, and still Raf couldn't forget Hank Harney. One evening he happened to pass the hotel where Hank had taken him. It was winter and Raf was on his way to a holiday party. Pine wreaths decked the doors to the hotel. Snow was showering down from the sky like fragments of clouds falling to the earth.

Of course, there had been several more men since Hank, a few dates. There was even a boyfriend for two years, a Japanese-American doctor who taught Raf to cook a Thanksgiving turkey and then left him for an online hookup.

But with the doctor, he had closure. And in a moment of truth, while alone in bed one night, contemplating his life, Raf could not deny that no one...no one...gave him the passion and the honesty that he had found with Hank. Raf and Hank had met as strangers. They had expected to part as strangers. So whatever they had to say could not be held against each other; they had nothing to hide. But something happened: too many caresses, too many kisses, too much...chemistry.

The consequence had been the most awkward good-bye Raf ever bid. When morning came, the two stood in front of the hotel, shoulder to shoulder, watching day illuminate the silvery sky. Snowflakes fell on them, soft as cotton balls, then broke into puffs of pinprick water drops.

"I had an amazing time," Hank said, turning his face to Raf.

"So did I," Raf said. "Good-bye."

They hugged, but they didn't kiss. They hugged for a long time. Then they let go.

Raf crossed the street to the trees lining Central Park. He turned around for one last look at Hank Harney. Hank was smiling his intoxicating smile, waving farewell.

Five years later Raf was on the very spot where they had stood.

Why didn't they exchange phone numbers and e-mail addresses? Why didn't he ask if Hank was available for breakfast? Why?

Raf was thirty-four years old now. He'd had more men than he had ever jacked off to when in college, experienced more adventures than he had ever witnessed in porn. Men came into his life with the serendipity of passengers on a plane. For the time that he was with them, they shared a common destination—the possibility of love. If the ride failed to live up to its promise, then it was over. No good-bye was necessary. No good-bye was merited.

Once in a while...once in a few precious moments that, with age, Raf was beginning to look back upon with bittersweet regret...he would meet a partner whose words and fucking sent him rocketing across the sky. He would say good-bye when what he truly wanted to say was: "Hello. Stay." He would say good-bye because as a man who loved men, he was a disciple of the tribal ritual of expressing love as a pleasure lavished on a myriad of his tribesmen rather than an emotion shared with one.

Yet Raf was not a man to dwell on regrets. He believed in the convergence of two lives that were meant to be united in harmony, and he believed in second chances. He believed in hope. Until he and Hank crossed paths again, he dealt with his loss the best way a man who gambled with love could.

Forget about him, Raf thought. *That Hank dude was just a bathhouse trick.*

THE CHAPERONES

Roscoe Hudson

James and I spent four weeks guiding a group of undergrads through Western Europe—four guys and three girls who spent their time praising *Abbey Road,* debating Marxism, guzzling beer and bed hopping. James taught history, I taught French and literature, and together we managed to keep the students from getting into serious trouble while hiding the fact that he and I had been fighting almost every day since we landed on the continent. We'd been teaching at the same university for three years yet no one knew we were gay aside from a few colleagues we considered close friends. Fewer knew we were married.

After a week touring Alsace-Lorraine our trip abroad concluded with a weekend in Brussels. James and I promised to take the students on a tour of the Royal Museums of Fine Arts, but by the time we arrived at our hotel they were tired, cranky and sick of visiting museums and cathedrals. Frankly, we were sick of them too. The only one who was eager to explore the city was Cliff. Neither James nor I nor any of the other students had ever seen Cliff on campus before. James told me Cliff burst into his office ten minutes before he was about to buy our plane tickets online. He tossed a white envelope full of cash on his desk and said, "Western Europe study abroad? Kick ass! Sign me up, man." Twenty-eight, with a bushy brown beard, green eyes and a brawny, toned physique, Cliff, whose usual outfit was a rumpled blue-and-white flannel shirt, frayed jeans and tan construction boots, looked more like a lumberjack than a college student. He claimed he enlisted in the army right out of high school, did tours in Iraq and Afghanistan then decided to get a couple of degrees in political science and comparative literature for the heck of it. The morning James and I met the students at O'Hare, Cliff arrived carrying only a dusty camouflage rucksack, an iPod and a battered paperback copy of *The Golden Bowl.* In no time he had managed to bed each of the girls on our trip, and subsequently broke each of their hearts. The guys revered him like he was their worldly older brother. He got drunk with them each night, took them to a hash bar in Amsterdam and regaled them with a story of how he killed two Taliban assassins with a single bullet in Afghanistan. After he got the boys kicked out of a bar in Metz for fighting with a Turkish patron, James contacted the registrar's office of our university and requested proof that Cliff was really enrolled in our school.

Regardless of his exploits, Cliff was as much a pleasure to look at as he was to have around. He was the subject of several fights between James and me, and over the course of the trip James's annoyance with Cliff became more and more obvious to the students. In Luxembourg we took the students for a tour of the American Memorial Cemetery and walked by ourselves through the rows of white crucifixes that served as headstones.

The students were observing the graves on their own. They followed Cliff, who had brought a small bouquet of flowers to place at the grave of his great uncle.

"The kids keep asking me what your problem with Cliff is," I told James.

He thumbed through his guidebook. "My problem," he said gruffly, "is that you want to suck his dick."

"Stop being crazy."

"You're always checking him out, Henry. I saw you eye-raping him when he came back from running yesterday. Your eyes were glued to his pecs. He's got everything you like: thick thighs, wide back, hairy all over."

There was no way I could deny checking out Cliff. He had a magnificent body that was impossible to ignore.

James rammed his guidebook into his backpack. "I thought we decided we weren't going to be like other gay couples, Henry. You promised me when we got married that it would be just you and me in our bed, no one else."

"I've been completely faithful to you, James. Where is all of this coming from?"

He turned his back to me and looked off into the distance at Patton's grave. In the distance I could see Marcy, Cliff's latest conquest, rest her head on his shoulder as the whole group huddled around him and looked mournfully at his uncle's cross.

"I'm turning fifty soon, Henry. I can't compete with a guy as hot as Cliff."

Hearing James make this confession puzzled me. After seven years I was just as attracted to him as the day we met. His elegantly tousled black hair began to gray three years ago, making him look more distinguished. He was broader and more muscular than Cliff, with a firm hirsute body I couldn't resist, especially after his workouts left him sweaty and funky. Feeling the soft hairs of his torso rub against my penis as he lay on top of me and plunged his cock into my hole was sheer ecstasy.

Incredulous, I stood in front of him with my mouth agape, my eyes darting back and forth. "What are you talking about, James? You hit the gym more than anybody I know. I love your body, baby." I tried to hold his hand but he pulled away and looked over his shoulder at the kids. "Christ, James, they aren't going to throw up if they see us holding hands. We've been sleeping in the same room the entire trip. They're not stupid."

James and I barely spoke until our train arrived in Brussels three days later.

With Cliff in tow we left the kids in their hotel rooms and decided to explore Brussels on our own. The three of us spent a couple of hours in the Royal Museums of Fine Art then wandered through downtown Brussels, took photographs of various buildings and narrow gray alleys, ate waffles coated in melted dark chocolate and confectioner's sugar and recounted our experiences on the trip. We were about to head to the Metro station to catch a train back to the hotel when Cliff suggested we all go for beer.

"Nah," James said as he flipped through his guidebook. "We should probably get back to the hotel and grab some sleep. Our flight back to Chicago is pretty early in the morning."

"C'mon!" Cliff said. He walked between us nibbling the last of his chocolate waffle. He had taken off his flannel shirt and tied the sleeves around his waist. His ample rump was covered but the tight white T-shirt he wore showed off his sinewy biceps. "When will we ever have another chance to get drunk in Brussels together?" He grinned and gave James a pat on his back.

"Henry and I should check on the kids."

Cliff scoffed. "Those kids are back at the hotel watching some crap reality show in Dutch. I say we toss back beers 'til dawn and stagger onto the plane. Do it up rock star, right Henry?" He winked at me and squeezed my shoulder. He was the only student who called us by our first names.

"We don't have to stay all night, James," I said. "Just a quick beer. Gotta have a beer in Brussels, right?"

"There you go," Cliff said. "You're outvoted, James."

Rolling his eyes, James put his guidebook back into his backpack. "Just one beer. Then we really need to go."

We strolled around downtown Brussels until we eventually found a bar across the street from an upscale casino. A rainbow flag billowed over the door and a small black placard with the club's name etched in gold letters, DUQUESNOY, shined on the crimson brick façade in the fading amber twilight.

"Looks like a cool place," Cliff said. "Let's try it."

James frowned at me. Persuading him to drink with a student was a huge effort in itself, the sixth of his personal Seven Deadly Sins of Teaching that he never broke. Drinking with a student in a gay bar was number seven.

"I don't know, Cliff," James said. "Maybe we can find someplace closer to the Metro."

Cliff smiled and said, "Guys, it's cool. I've been in gay bars before."

Cliff opened the door. A Nicki Minaj song thumped in our ears. A heavy black curtain blocked the entrance. Once we passed through we found ourselves in a small bar with a spiral staircase in the rear. Four men, pale and dumpy as dough, sat at the bar; they were all dressed in their underwear and athletic shoes. A sign above them, written in both French and Dutch, explained everything:

DUQUESNOY RULES

ALL PATRONS MUST WEAR A TOWEL OR UNDERWEAR ONLY.

ALL VALUABLES MUST BE LOCKED IN OUR STORAGE BOXES.

MUST BE 21 YEARS OR OLDER TO ENTER.

DO NOT PARK ON VANDERMEER STREET. YOU WILL BE TOWED.

PLAY SAFE—USE CONDOMS

James pointed to the sign and asked me what it read. When I told him his face tensed. He squeezed the shoulder strap of his backpack. "No way are we staying here."

The bartender, a short old man who looked like Mr. Magoo, pointed at the staircase. "Coming in or what?" he barked in French. When I looked at him closer I noticed one of his eyes was glass. *The Sopranos* played on a thirteen-inch black-and-white TV behind him.

"How much?" I asked.

"How about you show me an ID first?"

I stepped to the bar and flashed my passport. The old guy barely looked at it.

"What are you doing, Henry?" James said. "I told you we're leaving."

"Chill, James," Cliff said. "It's no problem. All we're gonna do is drink."

"This is not the place for us to be, Cliff. Not here with you."

"I look like Queen Elizabeth or something? Henry, ask him if we gotta strip down just to drink?"

I asked and the bartender replied yes, we had to be in our underwear. James's face had become tomato red at this point. He was slowly backing up toward the exit.

After I asked him about the dress code, the bartender added:

"Thirty euros for six hours. Eighty for a room. Extra towels are two euros apiece." Then he pointed at the spiral staircase again.

Cliff stared at James and me and, a bit fed up with our ambivalence, sighed and shrugged. "Well, you guys decide if you want to stay or not. I'm going up." And with that Cliff trotted upstairs.

James' face was contorted in an expression that could have been anger or sorrow. He clenched his jaw; his eyes reddened. "You want to stay, don't you?"

I never lied to him. "We don't have to play. We can just watch."

"What about Cliff?"

"This isn't about him. I want to be closer to you."

We hugged each other tight.

"I love you."

"I love you."

James held my hand and led me up the spiral staircase into the vast darkness above.

I took sixty euros out of my wallet and placed the money on the counter.

The bald guy behind the counter, shirtless and dark eyed with oversized ears stood about six feet five inches. A thick silver bead ring hung in each of his nipples. Geometric tribal tattoos covered his delts. "Gimme your wallet and shit, fella," he said in French. "It won't get stolen back here. We lock it all up."

The wall behind him was covered floor to ceiling with small black compartments. He pulled two long slender black boxes out, opened them and placed them before us. James and I put our wallets, cell phones and keys inside then the bald guy locked the boxes, put them back in their slots and passed each of us a key and a white bath towel.

The bald guy scratched his chin and eyed me curiously for a moment. "Out by midnight," he said. He hit a buzzer and a door to my right opened. In English he mumbled. "They're going to love the fuck out of you two." A creepy smile spread across his face.

James and I rounded a corner and entered a locker room. The only person there was a paunchy middle-aged guy with thinning brown hair and glasses. He was getting dressed. He looked me up and down before he put his blue T-shirt and ball cap back. Once dressed, he pitched his towel down a metal chute to his left and exited through the same door James and I came in. Our lockers were in the rear of the room. I stripped naked, locked up my clothes and wrapped my towel around my waist. James, somewhat reluctantly, did the same.

The whole building should have been condemned. Plaster fell out of the graffiti-covered walls. The cement floors were icy cold. Every time I took a step I thought I was stepping in semen, but it was only my imagination. Beyond the locker room area was a brightly lit communal shower. Four men were soaping up and stroking their hard-ons. Beyond the showers and the locker room was a wide straight stairway like something out of *Gone with the Wind*. Two young guys, heavily tattooed, sat on one of the high stairs and took turns blowing each other while a portly man stood over them and masturbated beneath his towel. They ogled us as we passed, and the portly guy tried to grab my arm. James and I held hands, ignored him and kept walking. Cliff was nowhere to be found.

Once we made it to the landing we walked through a pair of double doors and found ourselves inside a large theater. A gay porn flick was playing on the screen—an orgy with six smooth Asian guys going at each other in various positions. About a dozen guys sat in the rickety old seats watching it. As we left the theater I heard a voice in one of the corners near the door ask to suck my dick. James and I kept walking.

A staircase beside the theater led down to a dark amphitheater. Five monitors were suspended above, each showing a different porn film: one gay, one straight, one featuring black men, one bareback leather gang bang and one with frat boys. Five guys fucked each other with gusto on the top row of the amphitheater while three other guys formed a triangle at the bottom and sucked each other off. A few of them stopped to look at us, and one of the guys in the orgy on the top row waved James over. When the lights suddenly came on and a janitor entered the area pushing a cleaning cart, the men hastily covered themselves with their towels and scattered like roaches.

We left the amphitheater and trekked down a circuitous hallway, passing a long row of private rooms. Half were closed. In the open rooms, guys either lay in bed and jerked off or kneeled on the bed with their asses hiked in the air, condom and lube adorning the nightstand beside them, waiting for an anonymous cock. Still, no Cliff.

After a few turns the hallway got so dark I could barely see. I tripped over something, looked down and saw some guy's leg. He was on his knees in front of a glory hole. Once my eyes became accustomed to the darkness I realized where I was. Ten men were lined along either side of the hall in front of glory holes. Six of them were on their knees giving blow jobs and the others stood in front of the holes. A cacophony of grunts, moans and slurps filled my ears. I could feel a few random hands caress my back and legs, but I brushed them all off and kept walking behind James.

The corridor became a bit brighter. We stopped walking and stood in the doorway of a common area. Three monitors on the wall to my left played porn while five men sat on benches drinking sodas and chatting. Two vending machines—one dispensing soft drinks, the other condoms, lube, cock rings and poppers—stood near the entrance to another dim hall. I stood there thinking we would never find Cliff when I spotted him crossing the common area dressed only in a towel. The other five men cruised him as he passed. One of them whistled at him.

James and I followed Cliff down the dimly lit hall. We turned left, passed more private rooms and more men fucking with savage abandon. I followed James through another common area and into a small room illuminated by a light so dim I could hardly see. I might as well have been blind. I could feel James's presence, hear him breathing and smell his scent. Then he stopped abruptly and I walked right into him. I reached out, wrapped my arms around his waist and pulled him close. He grabbed my ass and squeezed it. Suddenly I felt someone kiss my shoulder. From the furriness of his face I knew it had to be Cliff. His mouth closed over mine. Then he kissed James. Then James kissed me. We caressed one another's bodies. Our dicks were hard as iron.

"Cruising for some Daddy dick, boy?" James growled at me. The register of his voice lowered to a depth so low it sounded bestial. He had never spoken like this before. We never engaged in role-play, and James had never expressed a desire to do it. His faced hardened, his nostrils flared, his brow furrowed. In the demi-glow of the open room, filled with the stench of cum, piss, poppers, marijuana, tobacco and musty bodies, my husband was as foreign to me as Brussels itself.

James leveled a cold stare at Cliff. "Daddy's been watching you, son. Been watching your hard muscle butt in those red shorts you run in. You been making Daddy think bad thoughts, boy."

Cliff kissed James. "I want your dick, Daddy." Then he gave me another soulful kiss. "I want you too, baby," he whispered to me.

We locked lips again.

James pinched my nipples then snatched my towel off and flung it somewhere into the vast darkness. He jerked my dick and gave my ass a good smack. "Daddy's big boy," he whispered to me. "Daddy's fucking muscle boy." He smacked my ass. "Need some dick in your ass, boy? Huh? Need some Daddy lovin'?"

I went "Uh-hmm."

"Good. Daddy's gonna stick both your jock asses."

James rammed his tongue into my mouth and placed a hand on my shoulder. He pushed me to my knees and I sucked his cock with gusto. His pubic hairs tickled my nose.

"Smell Daddy's crotch sweat. That's all piss and precum and sweat, boy. Slurp on Daddy's big dick."

The thrill of James's long fat cock stuffed in my mouth sent hot waves of lust throughout my body. His dick was so large it made my jaw ache, but I was used to it. Cliff joined me on the ground and licked James's balls. Occasionally one of us grunted. I jerked my dick, reached over and started jerking off Cliff too.

"Daddy's fucking slut boys," James groaned. "Good boys. You got Daddy leaking precum. Getting Daddy's juices flowing."

James grabbed his dick at the base and started shoving it to the back of my throat. I reached up, squeezed his pecs and pinched his nipples.

"Stand your ass up, boy."

I did.

"Turn around."

I did.

"Now stick out your ass."

When I bent over, James's thick, strong hands spread my asscheeks as far as they could go. He started rimming my hole, licking it in quick swirls before he slid his tongue into my pucker. He managed to get his tongue pretty far up my ass. While he was tongue-fucking me he kept squeezing my ass. Then he stopped rimming me, stood, bent over and kissed me. I felt his dick sliding up and down my asscrack.

"Daddy likes rubbing your sweet ass with his big dick. Daddy's gonna split his boy's ass wide open. Want me to pound my jizz up your guts?"

"Yeah, baby," I answered.

He gave me another slap and told me to hoist my ass in the air higher. He spit in my crack a couple of times and dry-humped me again.

"Get on down, boy."

When I got down on my hands and knees James squatted behind me and slid a finger into my ass.

"Fucking tight as hell," he said. "Daddy's dick is gonna hurt you, boy."

Another finger entered my anus. I clenched my asshole around them. I could hear James shucking on his dick. He probed my ass deeper and deeper until he found my prostate and rubbed it. I bellowed and arched my back. Cliff stood beside us and jerked off.

"Daddy's boy loves getting finger-fucked. Getting your ass ready for Daddy's horse cock."

James mounted me and pushed his large dickhead into my ass. I winced and sucked in a large breath. It felt like James had stabbed me.

He began to slowly work his cock in and out of me.

"Feel that dick, baby? Feel Daddy lovin' you?"

Eventually I became accustomed to his cock and moaned.

He held on to my hips and slammed his cock in and out of my ass at a moderate pace. My flesh became hot and sweaty. James increased his thrusting and his big mushroom head crashed against my prostate rapidly. My arms and legs trembled from the superfast fuck James was giving me. The alternate sensations of pleasure and pain seemed unbearable, and I couldn't help screaming and shedding a few tears. Cliff positioned himself in front of me and stuck his chubby cock in my mouth.

"Yeah, baby!" James cried. "Raping your ass, boy."

He pushed me down and pressed my face against the cold concrete floor while he mercilessly rammed ass. The sound of our bodies smacking together in the darkness drowned out the throbbing of my heart. James's hard pounding felt like a thousand brick walls were falling on top of me. Then James stopped fucking me, looked up at Cliff and gestured for me to move out of the way. He snapped his fingers at Cliff and pointed to the space where he fucked me.

"Your turn now, boy," James barked. "Get down here."

Cliff got on his knees but James rolled him over onto his back. Cliff raised his hips and held on to my ankles as James plunged his cock into him. Cliff gasped and bit his lip.

"You like getting fucked like this?" James asked.

Cliff moaned.

I lowered myself and stuck my cock into Cliff's mouth. James kept pummeling his asshole; his sweat drenched him. Cliff licked my cock back and forth. The harder James fucked him the harder he sucked me off. I couldn't hold back any longer—I shot my load in his mouth. Drops of my cum jeweled Cliff's soft beard.

"Yeah," James shouted. "Bust your nut, baby."

James kept thrusting into Cliff. The stench of their fucking engulfed the room.

"Getting close, boy," James groaned. "Want some Daddy jizz?"

"Hell, yeah," Cliff whispered.

James pulled out, reared up on his knees, roared and shot five streams of cum over Cliff's body. Once he finished he walked over to me and took me in his arms. We looked down at Cliff as he lay languid on the cold cement floor. Even in the dim light I could see his furry body glisten with sweat and semen.

James and I found our towels. We covered ourselves and stared at each other. I gazed into my husband's eyes searching for some sign of how he felt about me, himself and what just happened. I began to tremble. Then James kissed my lips and pressed me close to him. We left the room, hand in hand, together.

EASY DICK

Jeff Funk

"Are you having fun?"

"Yeah."

The man gave the john an angry flush. "Well, I think it's *shitty*! But, hey, you're *having fun*," said the deep-voiced butch daddy in leather. He walked out to his friends, and I heard him say, "That *thing* in there is showing his dick."

Jeez, I thought. *How did he know I was cruising?* I wasn't that into him. I even wondered why he kept lingering before he asked his question. Then I remembered: the first time I'd cruised the toilets at the bar, I had scribbled on the chalkboard above the twin urinals: CHARCOAL HOODIE, BROWN JOHN DEERE CAP NEEDS HEAD.

Busted.

Since the police cracked down, the staff at the bar were pretty uptight about letting dudes do what comes naturally. Now everyone was so prissy and proper. The bar lost its soul when they took away cruising.

Shucks, these city slickers have a nasty way of talking that leaves a country boy bamboozled, I thought as I zipped up my jeans. *Funny that he's holding court next to the cruisy crapper. What the fuck does he expect?* I swear, the park fellas judge the bathroom cruisers, who judge the closet cases, and so forth, when *everyone's* getting *lots* of cock. And why not? Sucking dick has become my hobby; fuck, it's what relaxes me most.

I ignored the jerk as I walked past his group of goons. Then I shoved the push bar of the side door and took a deep breath of night air. *Fuck this*, I thought. *I need easy dick.*

I smoked to calm myself during the drive to the Works. Once there, I saw that the parking lot held more than a few Cadillacs, which probably belonged to older, well-to-do men. The foreign cars, Jeeps and SUVs told me there would be all types of guys to choose from, and I shuddered with anticipation from imagining what the dudes who owned these vehicles looked like. I caught a buzz, then locked my car, walked to the entrance and pulled open the door. The bathhouse feels like you're checking into prison. "Could I get a twelve-hour video room?" I said into the opening in the Plexiglas window while sliding my membership card under the divider. Strong bleach and some industrial-strength laundry detergent blasted my nostrils. The scent makes me hard whenever I smell it because I know that upstairs the smells are even better.

"You're lucky," the towel boy said. "Our maid, Jerry here, just finished cleaning a room. We're full up as of now. No more rooms after you, big guy."

"Convention in the city?"

"Yeah and the Colts game is tomorrow." He buzzed me inside, and when I got to the counter he slid a towel to me on top of which lay a key attached to a stretchy bracelet. "I gotcha in room seventy-five, honey. Checkout is one-forty-five."

I nodded my thanks. A strong mist of cologne clung to the air as I walked toward the stairway to the video rooms. The design of the bathhouse was eighties art-deco chic, with diamond-shaped mirrors lining the halls. The rest of the decoration was an odd array of rainbows, unicorns, studs, fairies and signs from leather bars in San Francisco and the Midwest.

As I drifted up the single flight and strode to my room, I heard grunts and moans emanating from a line of closed doors. There was a three-inch slot at the top of every room; in fact, none of the walls went all the way to the top. As I passed an open door, I smelled poppers and heard the man in there moaning like a baritone in an opera. *Vibrato from a dude. Wonder what that cocksucker's technique is like? Maybe I'll have to find that out for myself. Yessir!*

I swung open my room door and tossed my hat and towel onto the bed. I kicked off my shoes then padded to the bathroom for a piss before play. Three men were huddled together to my left at the end of the hallway. A muscular college boy was on his knees, sucking them off one by one. The standing men pulled on their buddies' cocks till their turn came to use the suck boy.

In the bathroom, cold tile made my toes tingle while I strutted over to the bank of urinals and boldly took the one smack next to a hairy fucker who was naked and had a thick dick—a *pud*, if ever I'd seen one.

"Hey," he said, with a distinct note of pleasure that I was joining him.

Fuck yes, I thought. "Hi, man. Have any fun tonight?"

"The steam room is outta control, boss."

"Yeah?" I looked down at his hard cock that could plug an asshole open wide. "And you didn't get *this* taken care of? That's a shame." I leered at it then knelt and flicked my tongue over his piss-wet dick. I pursed my lips primly and gave micro-kisses to the lips of his pisshole, a long big gash that looked like a slot into which a nickel could be inserted. Next I ran my tongue across that nice crack in his peter, lightly probing the hole for honey drops. They weren't hard to find. Buddy was leaking a steady flow of sexual anticipation, making for one juicy cock.

I gulped the head, grabbed it with the suction of my lips and bobbed my head, eliciting deep bass-timbre tones. I glanced up at him and was pleased to see that he was enjoying himself. He pushed his puffy lips toward his nose as if he were going to snarl like a wolf. He hissed hot air in beast-like grunts instead.

I curled my fingertips around his shaved medium-sized nuts and tugged on them while working my mouth over, around, under and up his cock shaft. I encircled my lips again then rushed forward on it, taking it all the way to the root. His reaction to my deep-throating made it worth the fact I gagged. *Jeez, this is a fine specimen,* I thought. I slurped down on it again, choking myself good on this fucker's thick pole.

"Yeah, *yeah,*" he said, twisting both of his nipples with his arms crossed over his chest. Blood surged up his shaft. I could feel it swim into his cockhead and plump it up till he was so engorged, it was hard to fit into my mouth. Just then, his loud growls echoed in the bathroom, blasting my ears as his cock squirted a thick stream. I gladly swallowed it all, thinking to myself, *Mmm, I needed to grab some life. I needed to taste it, boy.*

He then surprised me by *really* coming, which was accompanied by an ululation resembling a marine's war-hoop. He squirted, squirted again—sounding like he was in pain—then he milked out the last of his cum for me to lick. I suckled him gingerly because I knew that his glans was now sensitive, and I'm not a sadist blow buddy like some of these fuckers who keep wallowing your dick around in their mouths well after you're *entirely* spent.

"Thanks, man," he said, pulling his dick gently from my mouth.

I patted his hairy ass when he turned to leave the bathroom. "Hot," I said. I got up and could feel the imprint of the tile pattern imbued into the skin of my knees. I took a piss. Then as I washed my hands, I looked over at the chalkboard next to the hand dryer. Someone had written: ROOM #47 ISO BJ. Already, I felt at home.

The first thing I did when I got back to my room was turn on the TV. I tucked the porno guide to television next to the wastebasket. I stripped off my jeans and shucked my shirt to add to the pile.

I wrapped the towel the bathhouse provided around my waist. It was still warm from the laundry room downstairs. It felt soothing to my scrotum. I propped open the door then stretched out on the bed with my hand underneath the towel, fluffing my cock. While I'm fond of flaccid dicks, a woody is the all-around crowd-pleaser, and I wanted some attention paid to mine.

As I lay watching male figures coasting past my room, I had the peculiar feeling again that I was back in college, only *this place* was like a "dirty dormitory" where men getting each other off was not the exception; it was the *rule*.

A man stepped swiftly into my room. His shaking fingers roved my inner thigh, cock and balls. He pressed a finger to my pucker like he was pushing a button to get an elevator. He explored me more very softly. It was as if he didn't want to disturb my slumber, so I lay with my legs spread, not moving a muscle. I let him help himself. It felt heavenly, turning over the duties of pleasuring my dick to his manly, appreciative hands.

He touched my balls in a weird manner, as if he were at once dialing and examining each orb. He pinched a fleshy, wrinkled fold of my nut sac and pulled at my balls like they were toys.

Another guy stepped into the room. "Hey, friend," he said to the guy screwing with my nuts. "Whatcha got there?"

"He's got big fuckin' nuts, dude. See?"

"Yeah? Let me feel." He honked them like a clown horn. "Yep, them's some big potatoes."

"Hee, hee. *Potatoes*," said the pincher. He went back to his favorite trick with my balls and pulled them pretty damn hard.

"*Easy*," I said.

"But did you see his dick jump?" the third man said to the pincher. Then he said to me, "Hold that pose."

My stiff boner obeyed while he proceeded to give me an eager, yet toothy blow job. *One time in a dream*, I remembered, *I gave a guy a D-minus in cocksucking; I marked it in red in a grade book.* In spite of the scrapes from this Southern stocky guy, I almost shot a big nut-load. Only, I wasn't ready to squirt yet; the night was young. "I need a break, fellas," I said. Wordlessly, they scampered off to their next adventure.

Once I was alone in the room, I closed the door and sat for a moment. I took off my glasses and placed them next to the TV that was playing vintage gay porn. I wrapped myself in my towel, stepped out the door and journeyed down several sets of stairs to the basement level, which featured the showers and the notoriously cruisy steam room. There were rooms downstairs, too. As I walked past the sling room, I overheard a young man on his mobile phone. "Nobody in the world loves you the way *I do*, Melissa," he said.

Several muscle bears were sucking each other off in the showers, but there were still plenty of shower nozzles unoccupied. I stepped to one and adjusted the temperature till the water was comfortable. I scrubbed all of my stinky parts so I'd taste good for the fellas. When I was finished, I didn't bother toweling off; in fact, I hung my towel and entered the steam room.

It *smacked* into me—the thick misty air comprised of steam, semen, wet hair pasted in sweaty pits, saliva and the scent of dick. I took a moment to become acclimated to breathing such dense humidity. It was like deep-sea diving. The lights were off. Through the mist was a canvas of animated naked male flesh, which writhed en masse with the lust of heathens. Being nearsighted added to the illusion that I was *lost* in the blur of this enchanted chamber. Sweat dripped into my eyes, stinging them slightly.

A mouth encircled my dick. The man sucked me good. *Why don't you teach a master class on giving good head, buddy?*

A daddy with woodsman's whiskers moseyed up and gave me a lingering kiss. I clutched his hairy shoulders and ran my strong hands down the sweaty, lush bear fur on his taut torso. Woof Daddy reached for my cock and snapped the cockhead with his thumb and middle finger. I groaned as the pain washed out of me and merged into waves of pleasure. He flicked my dick once more then he went down on me and kissed it to make it all better. He tongued my nuts with his fur-framed maw. He kissed my balls. He licked both of them and mashed his beard against them.

The ever-changing male mass made a shift in movement like a migration of the herd. Suddenly seated, I opened my mouth and got stuffed with a blond's dick. He looked like a surfer to me. I slobbered on his wet meat, and though I couldn't see it, I'm pretty sure I put a smile on his face. I sucked with my eyelids shut as rivers streamed down my face and I felt like I was in the exotic tropics.

Woof Daddy tapped the surfer on the shoulder and said,

"Let my brother in there." I then felt a wet and sensual mouth sucking me. He was a young hairless version of Woof Daddy, the naughty, cocksucking, boy-next-door type. While my dick was getting well serviced, I grabbed hold of a cock for each hand—Woof Daddy's and the surfer dude's dicks—then stuffed my mouth full. *A variety of dick is the spice of life; that's what I've always believed.* Little bro below pampered my hard-on with a tongue that wound like a snake searching for prey. A rush pulsed through me, energizing my body. Multiple men always amps up the hotness of sex. It was blissful, basking in so much cock, wet skin, body hair, stinking pits and feet, bushy-bearded guys and smooth fellas, seasoned cocksucking gurus and fumbling beginners—all blending into a mix of men sexually bonding, working together and happy to help every man drain his balls dry. A big-dick dude came up and smacked my face with his member. It bounced off my nose, then he fit it between my dick-juicy lips. He needed some of my hot mouth, too. The taste of a different dick made me swoon.

While the haters at the bar were posing and judging each other and *not* getting blown, across the city a tribe of wet men in the darkness of the bathhouse basement were exploring easy dick.

THE AQUEDUCTS

T. Hitman

The elegant stone bridge between two of Rome's seven hills hovered out of focus in the new morning's mist, far beyond the walls of the private courtyard. The day broke deceptively bright; Quintus imagined the water flowing down the top channel of the aqueduct above the footbridge and arches as liquid gold rushing to nourish Campus Martius, quenching the center's thirst, filling its baths. Somewhere along the Aqua Virgo, testament to Rome's growing enlightenment, the cold sunlit water met flames and heated, steamed. The results, Quintus agreed as he wandered closer to the open-air bath, seemed a gift from the same gods he no longer believed in.

Quintus stepped out of his sandals and let his robes drop. Soft fabric puddled at his feet. Steam kissed the sensitive points on his naked body—his throat and ears, his nipples, his cock, hanging erect without shame. Two of his Plebeian servants hovered close by, one with drink, the other a towel for his Patrician master. Quintus caught their glances, which normally should have stoked his arousal. Through their previous worship of his body, both men had proven themselves worthy of rights denied to their societal class, though neither could hope for such privilege. In the days, perhaps the years to follow, Quintus sensed he would crave and even need their mouths upon his body in the absence of the one kiss he desired most.

"That will be all," he said, and waved the servants away, perhaps to enjoy pleasures with one another in private while the morning grew brighter, the water flowed down from distant mountain springs and the Empire's territories expanded with each new minute. "I have all that I need for now."

It was a lie. Still, he offered the men a smile. Lucius, the nearer of the two, nodded and bowed his head. Quintus waited for the servants to exit and then reached between his legs, fondled his agitated thickness and the heavy pair of balls beneath. The steam had made the one part of his male anatomy harden, whereas it had loosened the other. Quintus's balls seemed to reach halfway to his knees in their current state, partially liquefied in the light of this new day.

Caressing himself, Quintus moved toward the steps leading down into the pool and the misty water. Heat raced up his legs. Steam rose from the bath, hypnotic, a vision from a dream. And beyond the ghostly spirals, Quintus's eyes again sought the arches and curves of the Aqua Virgo, from which the water in the grotto originated.

Hubris briefly pulsed through his insides, unleashing a shiver down Quintus's spine in spite of the engulfing warmth. His cock transformed from flesh to iron. Moaning, he openly pleasured his cock, his focus on the aqueduct while his mind—and heart—wandered elsewhere. Some disconnected version of his ear registered the scuffle of footsteps across the courtyard stones behind him, though Quintus remained trapped within the shroud of his longing.

"Senator," said a commanding male voice at his back.

Quintus's fantasy shattered. He turned and saw Marcus Rex standing beyond the wisps of steam, his dream persisting in that one facet, its most powerful. The Roman soldier was dressed in basic *lorica:* his imperial helmet with its transverse crests, the baldric worn over one shoulder presently empty of sword, *balteus* belt fixed over red wool tunic, thick-soled *caligae* sandals on large, handsome feet. This vision proved more spectacular than even the Aqua Virgo at sunrise because, in addition to the many wonders of the man himself, this man had helped to construct the wonder upon which water, life and progress flowed into the city.

Quintus's smile returned. "Senator? Have we become so formal with one another that we now rely upon official titles? Am I to refer to you as 'General'?"

Marcus's lips, the lower slightly plumper than its twin on top, hardened. "You sent for me, Quintus?"

Quintus maneuvered to the edge of the pool, his cock riding atop the heated water, until he was close enough to Marcus to reach up and caress the magnificent muscles of the soldier's right leg. Marcus's calf, coated in coarse dark hair, tensed like his face.

"*Marcus,*" Quintus said, speaking the soldier's name in incantation.

He gazed up. Mist gone opaque in the glare of the new daylight attempted to shield the soldier's face, but the twin sapphire-blues of Marcus's eyes reached Quintus from somewhere between sky and earth.

"Quintus..." the other man whispered.

Quintus leaned over the tiled lip of the steam bath, kissed the tops of Marcus Rex's toes, inhaled the rich male scent of his sweat. The soldier reached down. Fingers raked through

Quintus's locks. In response, Quintus's hand walked higher, past the soldier's bent knee, up his thigh and higher, into the damp heat hidden by his uniform tunic. Marcus's balls hung loose and heavy as well. The soldier's cock, Quintus discovered, wasn't simply erect but aroused enough that it leaked. Marcus grunted something guttural. Quintus's touch came away wet. He suckled the soldier's water off his fingertips and judged it better than that flowing down through the Aqua Virgo.

Soldier repeated senator's name, attempted to rise, only Quintus's touch, again on the hair-covered muscles of Marcus's leg, kept the man poised in a respectful kneeling at the edge of the bathing pool.

"Wait," Quintus said. "Please stay with me."

"My time in Rome is short, Senator," said Marcus. Before Quintus could interject, the soldier corrected his address. "*Quintus*."

"Germania," Quintus said. The word tasted foul on his lips, a curse in contrast to the invocation of Marcus's name.

"I go with my legion, where the Senate has ordered me," Marcus said.

"I did not vote for this new war," Quintus said, nestling his cheek against the soldier's leg. "Mine was one of the few voices attempting reason."

"War against Germania is reasonable if the Empire is to expand," Marcus said.

This brought them eye to eye. "When our soldiers aren't fighting wars of expansion, they are tasked with building marvels such as that."

Quintus aimed a pointer toward the aqueduct rising in the distance beyond the curtains of steam. He tracked Marcus's gaze to the Aqua Virgo; wondered at the silent calculations in those sharp lenses; fell deeper in love with the man that had challenged all of his beliefs, social and religious, since the completion of the project; since life and water flowed down from sacred mountain springs, transforming Rome and Quintus alike.

Boldly, he fondled Marcus's cock, his memory relaying its details: the chestnut curls wreathed around its base, the veins on its shaft, its head in the shape of an arrow, the pungent noose of skin around tip. His were the balls of a soldier, a king. Dare Quintus think it? A *god*.

"I stood in the Temple of Jupiter, and I felt nothing," the senator confessed. "Nothing, save my devotion to you, Marcus. And after witnessing the truly divine, I am punished to lose you to the dark forests of Germania."

The soldier's brave expression cracked. Reaching down, Marcus seized hold of Quintus's face in both hands. Rough thumbs caressed soft cheeks. Then Marcus crushed their mouths together, and the effulgent sun burning above Rome was no longer the brightest power on earth. That honor belonged to the rapid gallop of Quintus's heart, fueling the surge of emotion through his blood.

Lips locked and, for a wondrous instant, Germania no longer existed. Mouths parted. Saying nothing, for words weren't required, Marcus began to disrobe, helmet first, then *lorica* and tunic, finally sandals. So tall, with his neat military haircut, the cross-pattern of fur superimposed over chest and midriff, more on balls, legs. Those legs were the finest Quintus had ever seen or sampled. Even the soldier's feet were superior to those on the marble statues of Mars, Neptune—Jupiter himself!—that had once inspired the young senator's devotion to the gods, as well as his erections. Their toes were carved from cold, unfeeling stone, no matter how much he or other worshippers wished to dream life into them. Hot blood flowed through the feet walking closer toward Quintus.

Marcus stepped into the water. Steam embraced the human-god's body, conjuring drops of sweat across his flesh. Quintus rose up from the bath and met Marcus at the bottom step. There, he licked the beads off the soldier's neck, chest and nipples.

"Quintus," groaned Marcus, his voice powerful, magical.

Quintus's mouth wandered to the damp hair beneath Marcus's right arm, a part of the soldier's body so rich with male scent. Marcus accommodated his exploration by lifting and tucking wrist behind neck. Muscles flexed. While Quintus inhaled and licked, his fingers sought the soldier's cock. Marcus moaned again, and Quintus soon found himself guided lower. Mouth replaced hand. Marcus's thickness vanished between Quintus's lips.

Germania didn't matter. Neither did Rome nor the Empire for that matter. As for the gods...Mars hadn't constructed these latest and greatest wonders of a modern and mostly-civilized world. If the God of War was truly up there, gazing down from some celestial mountaintop bower festooned with fig trees, olives and vast arbors of grapes, all he had wrought upon the world was conflict and suffering. Jupiter had not built the aqueducts. That boast owed to the hands of men.

One particular set due rightful respect for the labor and construction of the Aqua Virgo gripped the back of Quintus's head, drawing him closer and then away in a rhythmic back-and-forth motion. With each forward plunge, Marcus's cock entered his throat, and only the lush, fragrant curls of his pubis and the soldier's balls prevented it from traveling deeper. On the backward, the head of Marcus's erection rewarded him with its sacred taste and proof of the soldier's arousal. Quintus swallowed, tugged at Marcus's balls with one hand, pumped his own cock with the other. Water flowed down the Aqua Virgo. Steam wafted up from the bath in the senator's private courtyard. Daylight spilled across Rome and the known world.

"Turn around," Marcus commanded.

His two simple words thrilled Quintus, for he could read whole passages of meaning between them. Releasing Marcus's cock, he did as ordered, settling his elbows along the stone lip of the bath. Waiting through the next few seconds proved torturous. Eventually, the soldier's warm breath teased his most sensitive flesh. Tongue followed exhale, offering tentative licks. Quintus tightened and bit back a howl. Marcus held him by both hips, securing him to the earth, and pressed his mouth fully against Quintus's opening. The soldier feasted, and the senator was sure that he would either climax into the bath without further stimulation, or go quite mad from the glorious sensations unleashed throughout his core.

Right when Quintus couldn't stand the elation another moment, Marcus released him, but only to exchange cock for mouth. The snouted tip of the soldier's erection tested Quintus's opening. Marcus then claimed ownership of resistant territory, taking it by force as he and his legion would Germania in the campaign about to shatter the peace, perhaps ending everything else that mattered in the deal.

A moment of sharp pain reminded Quintus of that terrible possibility. But the pleasure that followed removed its specter. Marcus entered him, the thickness of the soldier's cock challenging boundaries and rewriting territorial lines. One of the hands on the senator's hips traveled higher, its arm wrapping around his chest. The second found Quintus's cock in the water and performed magic through firm, metered strokes.

Marcus leaned over him. Chest hair scraped Quintus's spine. Quintus unclenched the muscles of his opening, and Marcus thrust in fully, his balls gonging, slapping at the water, a melody seductive enough to charm even Neptune. Not that Neptune cared, or *was*.

"I love you, Quintus," Marcus said, washing the words across his ear on a warm breath scented with the senator's own flesh.

Quintus cried out a similar pledge between thrusts, not wanting their connection to end. But too soon, the soldier's strokes brought the senator to ecstasy and, inevitably, the soldier's movements filled Quintus with his blessed wetness.

Marcus pulled out of him. They kissed one final time before the magnificent image of the aqueduct, floating out of focus in the ghostly haze of drifting steam.

"Remember this, Marcus Rex," Quintus whispered, still holding on to the other man's arms. "The age of gods is nearing its end. In Germania, if you believe in anything, believe in *us*."

Marcus nodded. Then the soldier walked out of the bath, dressed in silence and was gone, lost beyond the steam.

SHOWTIME

Heidi Champa

My eyes were closed as I lay on the towel that covered the teakwood bench. The air was moist and hot and I was already sweating, the drips running onto the terry cloth below me. I'd never been to the steam room at the gym before. In fact, I'd avoided it altogether ever since I'd joined. Frankly, I never saw the point of getting even sweatier in a tiny room after getting sweaty at the gym. It always seemed like a worthless endeavor, a way to waste more time before getting a shower and heading home. Until Ty told me to meet him there. Naked. He was late, but that wasn't a surprise. I often waited for him, but the one time I'd shown up late for him, I couldn't sit down for days. The hand-shaped bruises on my ass stung for way longer than I thought they would.

I quickly unwrapped the towel from around my hips just as I heard the door to the steam room open and close, but Ty caught me. As much as I wanted to open my eyes and see the look on his face, I didn't. I wasn't supposed to. I didn't want to make things worse. His voice was calm, but I knew he was pissed. The edge in his tone couldn't be completely hidden.

"Are you feeling a little shy today, Nate? You know better than trying to hide that pretty cock of yours."

I heard soft footsteps getting closer until I sensed his shadow over my face, his bulky frame blocking the overhead light in the steam room. My eyes stayed closed, but I could feel my heart pounding, my cock stirring to life just knowing he was near. I hated that he had so much power over me, but craved it all the same. I cleared my throat before trying to talk but my voice still came out rusty.

"I just figured—"

"You figured you'd stay covered, just to be safe. In case someone came by who wasn't me. Didn't you?"

I nodded, my words failing me. Sweat ran off me, heat radiating off every inch of my body.

"What if I wanted someone else to see you, Nate? Maybe that was the whole point of asking you to be here, to show you off a little bit. Come on, don't you want to make me happy?"

Even though he was practically whispering, his voice got louder and I knew he was leaning over me. I squirmed, waiting for him to touch me, but he didn't.

"Next time I ask you to do something, you do it exactly the way I tell you. Understand me, Nate?"

His hand went around my neck, not exactly choking me, but making it hard to breathe. I grabbed his arm with both hands, even though I knew I shouldn't.

"Let go of me, Nate. You know better."

Slowly, I unwrapped my fingers from his wrist and forearm and lay them back at my sides. I tried to calm down, but I was practically wheezing trying to get enough air.

"Now, nod if you understand me, Nate."

I moved my head as much as he would allow with his hand still firmly around my neck.

"So, you'll be a good boy from now on?"

Again, I nodded, shaking my head up and down until I felt Ty's fingers release, and I gasped for oxygen. The warm air felt thick in my lungs, but it was better than the alternative. He was still touching me, but for the moment he was gentle. I relished each stroke of his fingers against my cheek, knowing his mood could change in a second, which it often did.

"Good. Now, we can get back down to business. And keep those eyes closed, Nate."

His fingers twined in my hair and yanked hard, as he pushed his cock into my mouth at the same time, muffling the cry of pain coming from my lips. He was anything but gentle as he fucked my face, shoving his cock deep down my throat before pulling almost all the way back out. My cock strained, desperate for attention, but I knew none would be forthcoming any time soon. I thought of all the things I could be doing with my hands at that moment, if only he would let me.

"That's it, Nate. Suck me nice and deep."

Ty said it like I had a choice in the matter, but I really didn't. Not that I was complaining. Doing what he told me always made me hotter than any steam room ever could. Just as suddenly as he had started fucking my mouth, his cock was gone, my head dropped back against the bench with a thud.

"Get up on your knees, Nate. And, keep those eyes closed."

I fumbled around on the bench in my imposed darkness and put my ass up in the air. My knees dug into the wood planks and Ty gave each cheek a resounding slap with his giant hands.

"Tell me you'll do whatever I want you to do, Nate."

I pressed my forehead against the wood and curled my hands into fists as his tongue plunged into my asshole, swirling circles around my rim.

"I'll...I'll do whatever you want. You know that, Ty."

"Just like always. Right, Nate?"

"Yes."

I croaked out the words, the humid air making my tongue feel like lead. He laughed, the sound dying quickly in the tiny space.

"That's right. I do know, Nate. And, now they do too. You heard that, right guys?"

My eyes flew open and settled on the two friends that he had brought with him to the steam room, both naked with their hard cocks in their hands. I recognized both of them, but I'd never actually met either of them before. Before I had time to panic or try and wiggle out from under his grasp, Ty spoke up, teasing my asshole with his finger while he talked. If I'd thought it was hot in the room before, it was downright stifling at that moment.

"Well, Nate. I think you know what I want you to do. I just hope we brought enough lube. Say hi to Ted and Lex, by the way."

The two guys, one blond and one brunet, got up off the bench and moved toward me until their cocks were mere inches from my face. I didn't really need to be told what to do, but I still waited until I was given my instructions.

"Well, what are you waiting for, Nate? Get a cock in your mouth."

The blond, Lex, took the chance to stake his claim and shoved his cock in my mouth, relegating Ted to second place. Ted then grabbed my hand and wrapped it around his cock and I began to jerk him off, trying to keep up the pace he seemed to want. Lex fucked my mouth just as roughly as Ty had, using a handful of my hair to keep me in place. Ty was lubing me up, the slide of his finger temporarily taking my attention away from the two studs in front of me. He always had to be the center of attention, even though he'd orchestrated the whole thing. I started pushing back against his probing digit, the pad of his finger pressing against my prostate on each pass. Ty yanked me back by my hair, leaving both Ted and Lex hanging.

"You wanna get fucked, don't you, Nate? You want all three of us to fuck your tight little ass, don't you?"

I didn't hesitate this time. Not that he didn't already know the answer, but he always made me basically beg for it. And I always did.

"Yes, god, yes. Fuck me. I want all of you."

Ty let me go and I was back on all fours, Ted shoving Lex aside for the moment and ramming his cock into my mouth. While I went back and forth between them, sucking each one's cock as long as the other would let me, Ty fucked my ass. Hard. His body slapped against mine, all of us sweating in the steamy heat. Lex and Ted got increasingly frenzied, neither very good at sharing my mouth. I just let them do it, spit running out of the corners of my mouth with each invasion from a huge cock. Ty slammed into me, doing his best to assert his dominance over the situation and trying to knock me off balance. I heard someone talking, but I didn't know if it was Lex or Ted.

"God, Ty. This kid sure can suck. But when do I get a turn with that ass you won't shut up about?"

"Fuck, dude. Give me another minute. Then, Lex, I swear he's all yours. At least until Ted wants his piece."

I braced myself on my elbows as Ty pounded my ass a few more times and then pulled out. If my mouth hadn't been full of cock, I'd have groaned in disappointment. I didn't have to wait long, as Lex jumped right up and moved behind me. Ty sat back, letting Ted work over my mouth and Lex pummel my ass. Sweat ran off me like rain as the steam in the room thickened, guttural moans filling the space. Lex fucked me almost as hard as Ty had, gripping my hips with thin, strong fingers. Ted slowed his pace way down, making sure each stroke of his cock hit the back of my throat. I wondered what Ty was doing. It wasn't like him to give up control, but even without being inside me, he still called all the shots. Another voice interrupted the proceedings; I couldn't see around the cock in my mouth, but from his words, I knew it was Ted.

"My turn, Lex."

My eyes met Ty's, who stood with his cock in his hand. In the moment before everything started again, Ty ran his thumb across my forehead, wiping a line of sweat away. I was about to say something to him, anything, when Lex got between us, his cock slipping between my open lips easily. Ted kept up his slow pace as he fucked my ass, totally different than Ty and Lex. After all the fast fucking, it was a welcome respite to have him do something a bit different. Just like the way he'd taken my mouth, each thrust was slow but powerful, making sure I felt every inch. While Lex fucked my mouth faster than I could keep up with, Ted moved at his own pace. My cock was painfully hard, but I knew better than to do anything about it just yet.

Ty's voice filled my ears, but I could barely concentrate on the words, my focus so stolen by the two friends he'd brought with him.

"I don't know about you two, but I'm getting close to coming. And, I'm sure our boy here is too."

Lex and Ted's replies were incoherent at best, but I found myself flipped on my back, with the three of them standing above me. Steam rose all around them and I let my vision go fuzzy. My hand rested on my thigh, fingers twitching at the thought of finally being able to come. Even though he was out of focus, I stared at Ty and waited for the words.

"You wanna come, don't you Nate?"

"Fuck, yeah Ty."

My eyes snapped back to normal and searched his baby blues for a sign.

"What's the magic word, Nate?"

"Please. God, please, Ty."

He shocked me when he leaned down and planted a kiss on my lips. He smiled at me before standing up and finally putting me out of my misery.

"Well, what are you waiting for Nate? We want to see the show."

I wrapped my hand around my cock, knowing it wouldn't take long for me to get off. Lex, Ted and Ty all joined me, jerking themselves off as I watched. The towel underneath me was soaking wet. I met Ty's gaze and twisted my fist around the head of my cock. That was all it took to send me over the edge, hot cum spurting out onto my wet stomach. My toes curled against the wood, my groans joining those of Ted and Lex, who both started coming on me within seconds of each other. They kissed each other when they were finished, but I quickly looked back to Ty, who was still jerking his fat cock. Everything else faded into the background as I focused on him, opening my mouth in preparation for Ty's explosion. He took the bait and shoved the head of his cock in my mouth, just in time for me to swallow his load.

Ty threw a towel at me and I began to clean up as Ted and Lex made their way out of the steam room. I sat up, my head swimming from the heat and what had just happened. My knees were wobbly when Ty dragged me to my feet, wrapping his huge arms around me, slapping my ass hard before he kissed me.

"Did you have fun, Nate?"

"Yeah. Always."

"Good. Now, let's hit the showers. Ted and Lex are waiting."

THE CHANGING MAN

Thom Wolf

Bryan's black swimming trunks were over twenty years old. As he hitched them up his chunky white thighs, struggling to get them over the hips, he groaned. They were tight around the groin and waist, pinching his balls inside an unforgiving pouch, while barely covering the beefy expanse of his ass. His buttocks spilled out the bottom, exposing several inches of cheek. It was getting close to two months since he had last been to the pool, but they used to fit better than this.

Bryan slung his gym bag into the locker, together with his shoes. Draping a towel across his shoulder, he headed toward the swimming pool. His bare feet slapped loudly over the wet tiles. His step was almost as heavy as his mood. Why hadn't he splashed out on a new pair of trunks? He felt out of shape and out of date; painfully conscious of the thickening spread of his waistline and how the worn fabric cut into the flesh of his once peachy arse.

It was seven o'clock on Friday night. Though the pool and

the baths were open until midnight, it was quiet. Most people had better things to do at the end of the week than hang around the tired town swimming pool, but for Bryan, Friday night was all he had; a few hours on his own when he could do just what he wanted to do.

A solitary lifeguard sat on duty at the deep end of the Olympic-length pool. In the water, two women in full-body bathing suits and skullcaps swam slowly down the right side of the pool in a cautious, head-above-water fashion. Bryan put his towel on a hook by the door and approached the pool. He was grateful for it being so quiet. He had made a promise to himself to lose a bit of weight and get back in shape over the next few weeks. But he didn't want an audience to watch him doing it.

He sat down at the edge of the pool and swung his feet over the side, flinching upon contact with the water. It was colder than he had expected. He plunged his legs in deeper, feeling the shock as the cold rose over his knees, all the way to midthigh. After a moment's hesitation, he took a deep breath and jumped from the ledge. The shock of cold water, enveloping him from his feet to his scalp, was only momentary. Kicking from the bottom, he resurfaced and launched himself into a powerful breaststroke down the full length of the pool. At the far end he executed a neat turn, before powering back down the lane.

Like so many other things in life, swimming was one of those pleasures that he rarely had time for. Since his divorce he had to spend more time at work. With his ex-wife's alimony, child support and two houses to pay for, many of the luxuries that he used to take for granted were beyond his means. He had to work hard just to keep it going. Weekends were for his children; he collected them at 10:00 a.m. on Saturday morning and kept them overnight before returning them to his ex-wife late on Sunday afternoon. Friday night was the only time he ever seemed to have for himself. Bryan had to fit his entire social life into those few precious hours after work each Friday. Sometimes he went out with friends, occasionally he had a date, some nights he just went to bed early and slept. And sometimes, like tonight, he tried to do some exercise at the pool.

Spurred on by the frustration and guilt, he plowed through the water, turning his head occasionally to catch a breath. He felt a burn through his shoulders as he hurled himself across the pool, clocking up the lengths: ten, twelve, sixteen, twenty. Bryan kept going, battling tiredness and pain, fighting through it, clearing his mind of everything but the task of swimming.

Forty minutes later, he felt as if every muscle and sinew in his body was aching. The effort of walking or stretching was a pain, but while his body suffered, Bryan felt a calmness of mind that came from physical exhaustion. He was pleased with himself; he had made a decent effort and tested his body. One session would not improve his fitness, but it was a beginning, something he intended to keep up.

Inside the men's locker room there was a modest bathhouse, comprised of a small steam room, a Jacuzzi, a lounge area and showers. It had seen better days. The twin sofas in the lounge were stained and split in several places. The facilities had been built over twenty years ago and showed little sign of having had much maintenance in all that time. The cream tiles were badly cracked and mildewed, missing entirely from some sections of the wall. A pungent odor issued from the drains that even a heavy-handed use of bleach failed to disguise. Bryan would usually forgo the unsatisfying benefits of the steam room, in favor of a quick shower and a hasty exit, but tonight, as his muscles screamed in protest from his swim, he decided to ease some of that tension in the wet heat.

He entered into a swirling cloud of steam and the heat seared his nostrils. Bryan blinked and waited for his eyes to get used to the swirling fog. The room was tiny, little more than six feet by six, with a narrow wooden bench running around three of the four walls. Stepping farther into the steam he realized he was alone.

Bryan was naked. He had only brought one towel with him and had left that in his locker so he would have something to dry himself on afterward. He never considered himself to be one of those men who paraded around locker rooms and baths, stark naked and shameless, letting it all hang out, but at this time of night, he didn't expect there would be too many people around to see him. That suited him fine. He was here for the benefit of his health, not to get his rocks off.

The heat of the bench caused him to flinch as he sat down, as scorching wood made contact with his soft white buttocks and scrotum. The temperature caused his balls to hang low in their sac. He gave them a tug and rearranged his ass into a more comfortable position. He wouldn't be able to take the heat for long.

As his body relaxed, and the pain in his muscles eased, he found he could bear the heat for longer than he had expected. It became quite pleasurable after a while and he could understand, better than before, the appeal of unwinding in these sweat-boxes. The warmth and the moisture soon began to affect him in a serious way. He felt more aware of his body. He moved his hands across his sweat-slicked skin. Over his stomach, which was not really as bad as he had thought it to be, across his chest, around his nipples, which he was surprised to find were hard and aroused. His cock too, had started to lengthen and swell and as he idly ran his fingers across its length, it rose to full hardness. Bryan felt a shameful sense of excitement, sitting in a public place with a raging hard-on.

The warmth had increased the sensitivity of his dick; as he trailed his fingertips down the underside, it twitched and leapt. His foreskin slowly unfurled, releasing his cockhead from its protective hood. Bryan pressed his fingers to the tiny opening and felt it ooze a sticky, viscous fluid. He put his finger in his mouth, tasting his precome; salty and nice. He sucked it clean.

The door of the steam room suddenly opened.

Guiltily, Bryan snatched his finger from his mouth and covered his hard-on with both hands. Through the gradually clearing steam, he saw the figure of a man in the doorway, with black skin and very broad, sporty shoulders. The man entered the room, closing the door behind him.

"Hey." He sat down on the bench, at a ninety-degree angle to Bryan.

Bryan cleared his throat and managed to say, "Hi." How much had the man seen? Anything? Nothing? The steam was pretty thick, even now he could make out very little of the stranger's features; just a broad face and very short hair. Bryan sat still, too afraid to move and reveal his erection.

"Got a boner?" the man said. "It happens to me all the time in here. Must be this heat."

Bryan laughed nervously, watching the man through the steam. He was younger than he appeared, a fact that had been disguised by his athletic build and confident gait. He had a handsome, open face with a wide mouth and white teeth that shone through the mist. Bryan guessed his age to be somewhere around twenty-three or -four. There was a very attractive quality about the younger man that made Bryan anxious.

"It's all pretty new to me," he admitted. "I don't usually bother to come in here."

Through the wraiths of shifting steam he could see that the young man was also naked. He sat very straight and upright, his legs spread wide, his cock frustratingly hidden in the mist. "I didn't think I recognized you. I'm JB." He leaned forward, extending his hand to shake.

"Bryan." He moved closer, taking the offered hand, and then suddenly there it was; his cock—big and hard—as thick as a grown man's wrist.

"You see," the young man said. "I told you the heat made me excited."

JB sat back against the wall, but as the steam cleared around his groin, Bryan saw him holding his cock in one hand, working it with a slow and steady stroke. There was no mistaking the come-on, though Bryan found it inexplicable. The man must have been twenty years his junior, so fit and handsome; why would he be interested in Bryan?

"Don't be shy," JB said, holding his stiff dick and waving it like a sword. "We could help each other out here."

Bryan swallowed. Despite the humidity his mouth was paper dry. "I can't," he said. "I can't take a chance on getting caught. I have too much to lose."

JB smiled warmly, not in fun. "Getting caught? The only people you're going to see in here tonight are after the very same thing as you and me: a piece of ass. The old guy who runs this place, he knows what goes on. As long as we're all done by midnight, he turns a blind eye." JB stood up and for the first time Bryan could fully appreciate the splendor of his body. This was a young man in his prime: strong and lithe with hard-earned muscle, a flat belly and a gargantuan dick. Bryan could barely breathe, looking at that body, that cock; the only thing he knew with any certainty was that he wanted it. He put out a hand. Trembling fingers moved closer to the slowly pulsating flesh. He touched it, cautiously feeling its heat and strength, before opening his hand and wrapping it around the shaft. He held JB's cock in a determined grip, aware of the fact that his thumb and fingers did not meet.

Before he knew what he was doing, JB's cock was in his mouth and he was kneeling on the hard, tiled floor, burning his knees as he struggled to stretch his jaw around the boy's massive black dick. Bryan's inhibitions were forgotten, as intangible as the swirling mist. He didn't care that they might be found, that he might lose his job or what was left of his family. He didn't care that the boy was so much younger than he was, so much fitter and more attractive. All that mattered was his cock: the size of it in his mouth, the taste of it, the force of it. In those moments it was everything.

Though he had had experience of sex with men before, it was limited to very casual exchanges—a quick hand job in the bathroom at Walmart or a hurried blow job among the trees that lined the back of the park. Bryan was no expert when it came to handling or sucking a cock. He didn't know the best techniques or methods. He relied on instinct and his instincts were good. He opened his jaw as wide as it would go and kept his teeth clear of the sensitive cockhead. It wasn't easy, not with a dick as big as this. He tried to suck and took it as far back as his mouth would allow. He almost felt insignificant, on his knees, taking JB in his mouth; the boy was like a god and Bryan didn't feel worthy.

Bryan was filled with a sense of wonder; being with a man felt strange to him, so wrong, and yet so wonderful. *I shouldn't be doing this,* he told himself. *I shouldn't be sucking this boy's cock!* But why not? It felt so good, so right. He loved it.

He held JB's balls, gently, in the palm of his hand, marveling at their size, their weight, the feel of their skin against his.

"Oh, man," the boy growled, "take it easy or I'm gonna pump my load down your throat any minute." He tapped Bryan on the shoulder. "Come up here a second. Let me look at you. I wanna kiss you."

It felt as though their roles had got mixed up. Shouldn't he, the man, be telling JB, the boy, what to do? Shouldn't JB be sucking his dick? A voice in his head told him no, that would be wrong. *Let the boy order you around. This is what you need.* Bryan rose. Face-to-face, JB was taller than him by a good five or six inches. Bryan submitted to the younger man's strength and size.

JB slipped his arms around Bryan and his hands went straight to his ass. Strong fingers dug into the malleable flesh, kneading it. He pulled Bryan's body close to his and lowered his head to kiss him fully on the mouth. Bryan opened his mouth to the kiss, allowing JB's tongue to roam around inside. The boy's cock, so big and wet, prodded against his belly. Bryan leaned into him, squashing their cocks together. His heart raced, stimulated by the heat of the room and the overwhelming sex of the young man.

"Shall we take this through to the lounge room?" JB asked, breaking the kiss. He ran a finger down the seam of Bryan's ass, gently probing the hole. "I can't fuck you in all this steam. We would both have a heart attack."

Fuck me! He wants to fuck me! Bryan panicked. *He wants to put that massive dick in my tiny asshole! No way can I take that thing, not in my ass!*

The cock throbbed against his belly. So big, so hard, so tempting and desirable. Bryan jiggled his ass in JB's hands. "I want you to fuck me," he said softly.

Like the rest of the facilities, the lounge area had seen better days, long, long ago. There were two tattered-looking sofas, with foam showing through the frayed edges, scattered with mismatched cushions. An old glass-topped coffee table stood in between the sofas, littered with an array of out-of-date magazines, while a thin, patterned curtain separated the lounge from the locker room. There was nobody else around, though Bryan drew the curtain closed behind them, shielding them from casual eyes. Music was piped in through a crappy PA system. It was the same generic rubbish they played in the gym and the pool, supposedly to inspire, though it did little more than irritate. It didn't matter; nothing could spoil the mood or deter the two men.

JB had entered the room ahead of him. He turned to face Bryan, smiling while his huge cock swayed at full mast. Bryan stared at the colossal shaft. *No way can I take that,* he thought. *That thing would fill up half my bowel.*

JB pointed at the sofa to his right. "Bend over there," he said. "Stick out your ass so I can eat it. I wanna get you all juicy and wet."

Once again Bryan found himself compliantly obeying orders, doing everything the younger man demanded of him. He knelt on the creaky sofa, rested his arms against the back and pushed out his ass, presenting himself to JB. Some men hesitate before getting up in another man's butt, but not JB. Planting a hand on each cheek, he rived Bryan's ass open, spreading it, stretching it.

"Sweet," he murmured, before moving in for his prize.

His tongue was hot and moist and Bryan let out an involuntary "Oh," as it stroked his crack from the bottom to the top. Bryan dug his fingers into the back of the sofa. The pleasure was unreal. His breath came in tiny gasps and he shuddered as JB tenderly caressed his asshole with his tongue. It was too much, too exquisite to be real. “Oh, man,” he moaned, focusing his entire being on that tiny, often-neglected area of his body. The experience was a revelation, something he had never known or imaged before.

JB took his time giving Bryan’s hole a lot of attention. It was as if he knew that this was new, virgin territory, and he wanted Bryan to savor it and enjoy it. When the hole began to relax, he pushed his tongue inside, working his spit into the passage. He inserted a finger and pushed his saliva deeper and deeper. “You think you can take me yet?” JB asked, rising to his feet.

Bryan looked up at him, over his shoulder. “I want to. I really want to.”

JB smiled. He spat into his hand and slathered it over the head of his cock. He spat again and stroked it down the shaft. Holding his cock near the base, he began to tap the head against Bryan’s asshole, anointing the opening with spit and precome. Bryan arched his back, giving up more. The hot and wet tap-tap of that dick against his ass was divine. When cock and hole were both juicy and wet, JB pressed more firmly. “Just relax,” he said. “Don’t fight it.”

Breathing through it, Bryan willed himself to relax as the thick head forced his tight, tiny opening apart. He felt himself stretch wider, farther—it seemed impossible. It hurt but he kept on going. *Oh, fuck, I’ll never be able to sit again.*

JB stroked the small of his back. The head was inside and he guided the rest into Bryan inch by inch, dividing those cheeks with his girth. Sweat ran into Bryan’s eyes. He was hotter now than he had been inside the steam room. JB held his hips and began a very slow roll, back and forth, moving his cock merely millimeters to begin. As Bryan’s butthole began to give up its resistance he withdrew a little farther, moved a little faster, until he was giving it to Bryan in a slow, screwing motion. "This okay for you, man?"

Bryan could barely speak. "Oh, yeah," he managed breathlessly. He was overwhelmed by the experience of being fucked this way. He had never surrendered himself so completely to pleasure. The dick in his ass was solely for him. While he was getting fucked there were no alimony payments to worry about, no child support or credit card bills to pay. He wasn't Bryan the ex-husband, or Bryan the father, he was just Bryan the bottom, getting fucked by a big young dick and loving it. The aches and pains, the ravages of age that had been such a concern earlier in the night, were forgotten. For the moment his world did not extend beyond his ass and the cock that was fucking it.

In and out, slick and smooth, JB's dick tore up his hole. They groaned and sighed, smashing their bodies together, dripping sweat. Bryan had lost his own erection. It didn't matter, his cock was not important; this was all about his ass. His slack genitals smacked against his belly, matching the rhythmic thrust into his rectum.

JB's thrusts became increasingly erratic. "Gonna shoot," he gasped. "Want it in you?"

"All the way."

JB slipped his hands beneath Bryan's waist, hitching his butt higher. He smashed it faster and faster, rabbit-fucking his juicy hole. With him giving a prolonged "Ohhh," his cock throbbed and spasmed, ejaculating his load in exquisitely long propulsions. His thrusts decreased to a very gentle slow screw until there was no motion at all. The two men gasped and heaved for breath.

Afterward, in the shower, Bryan could not stop smiling, though he kept his back to JB. Funny he should be shy now. The boy had known his body in the most intimate way imaginable;

there was nothing he could hide from him. Bryan stood beneath the almost scalding water and soaped his body. He was not the same man who had entered the pool just a couple of hours earlier. That was a very different man; he had not been fucked. He slid a soapy hand to his ass and touched himself. It was sticky and loose and sore; *oh, yes, this guy had definitely been fucked.*

Satisfied, sensual, desired—the new man was a big improvement on his predecessor.

WHAT I AM FOR

C. C. Williams

The auditorium buzzed with muted conversations. The attendees at the kickoff presentation of Grandville College's annual gay history series, Stonewall Consciousness, stilled and took their seats when the houselights flashed. Professor Ryan MacDonald mounted the stage and tapped the microphone. "Ladies and gentlemen, it is my pleasure to introduce our speaker tonight. Many of you know Doctor Stuyvesant from his hugely popular lectures in modern sociology. For those who don't, I guarantee you are in for an interesting—and perhaps shocking—experience. Without further ado, Doctor Gustav Stuyvesant."

Greeted by applause, rooting and cheers, Doctor Stuyvesant crossed the platform, his tall elegant frame trim in his signature three-piece navy-pinstripe suit. "Thank you, Professor MacDonald!" Removing the microphone from its stand, Stuyvesant walked around the podium to the front of the stage.

"Two hot, horny men fucked my face. They stood before me,

wrapped in humid mist, their swollen cocks invading my willing mouth. It was eleven o'clock in the morning..."

Wolf whistles, chuckles and a few gasps greeted his opening statement.

Stuyvesant surveyed the crowd, a broad grin splitting his strong handsome face. "That was over thirty years ago, and I remember it as if it happened last week. It was in fact a watershed event in the hesitant, scary process of my coming out. My very first trip to the baths!

"Young and almost totally inexperienced, I was visiting friends at Northwestern in the spring of nineteen-eighty. I knew that if I really wanted to find out what I was and what it meant to be gay, Chicago was certainly a much better place than the small town in Iowa where I was going to school at the time."

A chuckle ran through the crowd—Stuyvesant was a Grandville alumnus.

"I had found the address of the Country Club Baths in a ragged Midwest Mattachine newsletter and with stomach-churning anxiety took the L downtown. For almost an hour, I fidgeted up and down the street, psyching myself up to go in. Stubbing out my fifth cigarette and tightening my sphincter, I sailed through the door, hoping I exuded an attitude I didn't feel.

"My hand shaking, I shelled out five bucks for a compulsory membership and another five for admission and locker rental. The Country Club Baths was glitzy and steamy and smelled, even at that hour of the morning, deliciously of sex. A silent, faintly supercilious jockstrapped towel boy with sculpted glutes showed me my locker. He hung around, flexing and posing, obviously waiting for a tip. I flipped Adonis a quarter and mumbled, 'Thanks.' He stuffed the coin into the bulge of his jock and drifted away.

"Tearing off my clothes and flinging them into the tiny metal cube, I ogled the hot, sweltering parade of men, stalking and cruising with white towels draped at rakish angles from hunky hips to cover a variety of mysterious, exciting bulges. It was a hard-core candy store, and I was a hungry kid with a sweet tooth and money in his pocket.

"A thought hit me like a fist in the gut: I didn't know how to get the candy! I'd never even been to a gay bar, and here I was at a veritable sex fest and didn't know the rules. Hell! I wasn't even sure what the game was!"

Appreciative laughter echoed. Stuyvesant sipped from a water glass. "Remember—this was the early eighties, what you might call B-I—Before Internet!" He grew pensive, a frown crossing his face. "Even before AIDS. There were no openly gay people on television or gay issues regularly in the news—particularly in Iowa." He replaced the tumbler and resumed his pacing before the audience.

"Running around yanking towels would lack class, I decided, happy that my mind was still rational—even in my excited state. I recalled my two years of ROTC training. *Reconnoiter*, I thought to calm myself. The men passing through the locker area all headed toward a narrow stairwell leading into the depths of the club. I decided to fall in with the parade.

"A few steps downward steamy humidity glazed my skin; the joyful cascade of many showers susurrated upward. Pervading everything, a pungent integral part of the atmosphere, hung the wonderful biting aroma of raw sex.

"A brightly tiled archway at the bottom demarcated another world, a world of heat and water, a world of naked men. To my left lay a small pool where wet forms cavorted in the steaming, churning water; to my right a row of wooden white chaises, each occupied by one—or more—men in varying states of excitement or repose. Beyond them, once I dragged away my greedy eyes, stood a shower area. Sporting multiple spray heads arrayed about a gleaming stainless-steel phallus, the shower accommodated several men showering at once in full view of the other men. Since the round room was encased in thick glass, they also stood revealed to the pool and chaises. Past the showers was the steam room, strategically placed so one had to squeeze through, between and around the soapers and soapees to get to the action behind that door.

"I managed to wrestle my attention from all those bodies, all that cock, ass, soap, and glistening, gleaming flesh, and walked, as nonchalantly as I could, to the showers, acutely aware that my rambunctious cock already angled my towel out and up. Serious indecision struck when I reached to undo the towel at my waist. Not since my grade-school days at the YMCA had I been so publicly naked—and here I was with a bobbing erection just ready to bust loose, to burst free!

"To my chagrin I realized that not one of the men surrounding me was paying me any attention. The removal of my towel would not cause the slightest ripple on the surface of this seething pond. Amused by my own nonsense, I whipped away my towel and waded into the roundhouse.

"After an exciting squeeze between the hard bodies in the shower, where my cock was soaped by more than one pair of anonymous hands, I discovered the steam room—a Grecian-tiled chamber with a thigh-high ledge along the walls. Two men sat, one at each end eyeing the other, and caressed matching erections.

"No need for more recon, I thought. There was plenty of candy right here!

"I sat mid-shelf, equidistant between them—the tiles warm against my ass—aping their actions, rubbing my own rigid shaft. I glanced from one to the other as if I were at a tennis match. Innocently, with no realization of what I accomplished, my smiling acknowledgment of their wonderful cocks sent the perfect signal. As one, they moved to stand before me, two veined, throbbing spears bobbing just inches from my smile. Instinct took over; I opened wide and leaned forward. Simultaneously, the cocks invaded my mouth. Scarcely ten minutes had elapsed since I'd paid the money at the door!

"After the double-dong distraction of the steam room had come—and gone—I realized we had not been alone. A lone figure reclined in the foggy recesses of the upper marble tier, his flaccid cock resting against one thigh. I had no idea what the rules were. But gauging from how friendly the other guys had been with only the slightest encouragement, I approached the figure through the hot mist.

"He looked to be in his late twenties, six foot three, with a hairy chest and well-formed legs, all covered with gleaming sweat. His eyes were closed. A relaxed smile curled his lips as if he were well into a wet dream.

"I knelt below him, a major decision to be made—an important decision—a question of tactics. To grab his cock and balls might seem too forward; to tap him gently on the shoulder, not forward enough. With a panting anxiety, I chose a middle path. I reached out and rested my hand gently but firmly on his muscular thigh.

"The man's eyes opened slightly. I met his gaze. He closed his eyes again and, still smiling, parted his thighs. That was all the affirmation I needed. I took the thickening cock between my lips and sucked it into my salivating mouth.

"Later, after the silent man climaxed, I staggered back to the showers, prune puckered, sweat slick and gasping for dry, unheated air. Exhilarated, I had overcome my anxiety—I'd savored the delights of the humid, sultry depths of the club—I was now ready to scale the heights!

"Back up on the first floor I discovered the snack bar. Three or four towel-clad figures sat at separate glass-topped tables drinking soda or coffee and munching junk food from machines.

"*Nothing exciting here,* I thought. Ready for more action, I began to leave, but a rumble in my belly stopped me. My breakfast—three cups of coffee, two cigarettes and a joint—had long since left through my pores. I returned to my locker to get change for a Coke and a snack. Processed sugar in hand, I sat and eyeballed the trade in the room. One bite into my Milky Way, I saw him!"

Stuyvesant paused dramatically, miming a half-taken bite of a candy bar.

"The angle of his towel, slung low on one hip, left very little to the imagination. Yet the extravagance of that package indicated there was grand and monumental treasure hidden beneath. Perhaps thirty, he looked Mediterranean: olive skin, dark curls and a muscular chest covered with a lush, sable pelt. I was interested—scared—but interested. My cock stirred beneath my towel. *What to do next?*

"The man, coffee in hand, turned from the machine to survey the room. Our eyes connected—locked, I dare say! He smiled. I was already smiling. A smile, I had deduced, was an important commodity at the club.

"The man sat across the glass top from me. 'Hi! I'm Tony.'

"I glanced down; the split in his towel gaped, exposing more of his exciting upper thigh. I took a swallow of my pop. 'I'm Gus.' I realized that—even though I'd already had sex with three men—those were the first words I'd uttered since I'd tipped the towel boy.

"'Come here often?'

"'My first time,' I answered quickly—and honestly.

"'Where do you usually go?'

"'My first time—ever!' I blurted.

"'Christ! A virgin!' Tony whistled, loud enough only for me to hear. 'Jeez, would I like to show you the ropes!' Tony's enthusiasm was positively boyish. My fantasies ran wild! Tony with his hard cock fucking my face. Me fucking him, him coming across my chest, my cock...

"Then I realized that Tony was still talking.

"'This isn't good for me,' he was saying, 'but I still love it!'

"'The baths?' I asked.

"'Oh, no!' he answered, as if he were surprised by the question. 'The coffee. All this caffeine gives me the shakes by the end of the day.' He paused, reflecting. 'The baths,' he gestured to include more than the snack bar, 'the baths keep me from going nuts!'

"He didn't seem to require a response. He just kept talking, all the while eyeing my crotch through the glass tabletop and running his fingers along his own naked thigh.

"'I really shouldn't be here at all,' he continued. 'I mean, what the hell would the wife say?' His laugh displayed no hint of nerves, just a sense of the ridiculousness. 'I mean, I love her—my wife—and my kids too. I ought to be at work. That's where my wife thinks I am. I told my secretary I wasn't feeling well and was going to take an early lunch, so I would be out for a few hours. But not to tell my wife if she called—didn't want her to worry. I do this about once a month.' He paused, smiled. 'I could get away with coming here more often, but, what the hell, why take chances? You know what I mean?' He paused again. 'Christ, I love dick!'

"His entire fist was now inside his towel. I eyed the bulge, so apparent before; it had grown—abundantly. I was so busy watching, mentally measuring his hidden cock; I had stopped listening momentarily, until I heard the words 'Come to my room.'

"'Huh?'

"'My room. Would you like to come to my room?'

"'Sure.' Sounding more confident than I actually felt, I was pretty sure I wanted to go, but I wasn't totally certain. What would going to his room entail? Fuck it! I wanted to experience the whole place, didn't I? And I certainly wanted to experience Tony! 'Sure. Let's go.'

"Tony stood, unconcerned that his towel led the way. We left the snack bar, the envious eyes of every man there moving first to Tony's tented crotch, then to my smiling face.

"Tony's room, one of several along the half-lit hallways that snaked through the upper floors, contained a bunk and only enough room to change one's mind.

"'Lock the door.' Tony jerked the towel from his hips and draped it over the bare lightbulb to soften its harsh glow. His voice had a different quality now—more urgent, more demanding. 'I don't want us interrupted.'

"In the half-light we faced each other naked and erect, eyes hungrily locked. Finally I wrenched my gaze away and appraised his hot body, even hotter than those snack-bar fantasies. While I consumed Tony with my eyes, his cock, deliciously uncut, jerked and bobbed, getting harder. With no further encouragement I dropped to my knees and captured that swelling between my lips.

"'Oh, fuck, yes! Yes!' Tony groaned. His strong, thick-fingered hands grabbed my head to keep my mouth from plunging down the length of his shaft. He held me fast, his foreskin barely touching my lips. I darted my tongue forward, licking gently at the tip of his cock. It grew harder, thicker. I forced my tongue under the fleshy cowl and circled the hot crown.

"'Oh, fuck!' Tony moaned and pushed forward. The head of his dick emerged from its slippery sheath. The salty, slightly bitter taste of his cockhead filled my mouth, exciting me. I moaned and rubbed my own cock, now rigid between my splayed thighs. Tony pulled me to my feet, his powerful hands still clutching my head. He stared into my eyes for long seconds and then drew my face toward him. His mouth was sweet as he licked his own cock essence from my eager tongue. His hands descended across my chest and belly until they captured my cock and balls, stroking and caressing.

"He laid me back onto the bunk, standing over me for a minute; then, kneeling between my legs, he leaned forward and began to kiss me again. To lick me. To devour my face. I felt his tongue against my eyelids. Christ, it felt good! Then my nose. Tony's tongue moved in hot tingling circles. Down my neck his mouth coursed, chewing softly, to my nipples. Down. Down.

"Tony's tongue slathered the base of my cock and slid yet farther. I moaned at the hot, searing touch against the tender skin over my balls. Gently Tony sucked one ball into his mouth. I groaned. Then, slowly, just as gently, he sucked in my other ball and began with his tongue, his lips and throat to squeeze them, massage them, bringing me to the brink of orgasm. Finally the massaging ceased. Tony freed my aching balls from his hot mouth.

"Before I could recover my breath, Tony's scorching tongue slid around the tip of my cock; and he sucked me into the heat of his wonderful mouth. Teeth and tongue welcomed me, exploring the contours of my shaft. Its length disappeared into his mouth and down his throat. His humming buzzed against my sensitive cock.

"Crazed by his mouth, I pumped my cock into Tony's face. I moaned and moaned. Tony grabbed my balls and squeezed gently, taking me deeper and deeper into his throat. Suddenly, he released my cock. Again his powerful hands lifted—this time my legs and hips. He buried his face in my upturned butt, his tongue flicking in and out of my burning asshole.

"'Oh, yes!' Never had I felt anything so wonderful, so sublime! I begged for more, and Tony answered, ramming his tongue in, jamming it down, twisting, turning, curling against the screaming, hot tender flesh inside me.

"'I'm coming, I'm coming!' I crooned, beyond wanting to control my cock.

"Reaching around my hips and forcing his tongue deeper inside me, Tony massaged and squeezed my rod. All of a sudden, a searing load burned out of my shaft. Come spurted against my eyelids, up my nose, into my gaping, gasping mouth. I'd never tasted my own essence before. Tony smeared it across my hungry lips—excitingly bitter, excitingly sweet. Before I could react, Tony removed his tongue and pressed the head of his cock against my slathered hole.

"A sharp flash of pain bit as the head stretched my hole wider. I was still spurting come when my complaining ring relaxed and yielded before the gentle force of Tony's cock. It slid slowly inward, filling me.

"'Oh, yeah. Fuck yeah!'

"That lengthy cock pushed deeper and deeper inside me, burning me with pleasure. My cock, still inches above me, jerked hot drops onto my lips. Tony's balls slapped against my ass as he slid entirely inside me. He began to withdraw, every inch sending icy shivers through my hot sphincter.

"'Oh, what a sweet ass!' Tony fucked me slowly, then slower, then fast. Then faster still and harder! Oh, so hard! His hips hammered my ass. His breath hissed between clenched teeth. He stifled a scream, and his cock stiffened within me and swelled even more. I bucked my ass to meet his final wracking thrusts, and he came, his whole body jerking! Groaning from the center of his being, he shot jets of come into my rocking ass.

"Then I felt that familiar hot tightening of my own belly. Without my touching it, my cock exploded again, spurting another load onto my ready, greedy lips.

"Two exquisite hours after entering Tony's room, I staggered out—in love with Tony, in love with the club, in love with my own body, in love with being gay, in love with hot, casual sex. I headed for the shower. The hot, tingling cascade in the roundhouse relieved my fatigue. The sight of three men lathering up went straight to my crotch. I overheard a comment: 'Jesus, the orgy room is hot today!'

"Orgy room! Where?"

Stuyvesant swiveled his head and craned his neck. Laughter bubbled through the audience.

"The only floor I hadn't checked out yet was the top one. I tore my gaze away from the rhythmic cock soaping next to me, fled the showers, and headed for the stairs.

"The orgy room was dark—and hot! As I parted the heavy black leather flaps that curtained the entrance, moist heat laden with the musk of healthy, sweating men surrounded me. Unseen fingers touched, rubbed and caressed me. Before my eyes had adjusted to the blackness, my cock was slurped into the satin cave of a hot mouth. It was an X-rated fun house! My vision improved; a writhing mass confronted me. Men pumping, jerking, sucking, rubbing and, of course, men fucking. Ah, the aroma, the closeness, the heat, the wetness! The wonderful sounds—sharp cries, groans! I surrendered to all of it.

"I waded into that dark moil. Hands and bellies, thighs and lips and tongues, buns and balls and cocks—all writhed about me. Awash in sensation, my entire body was a raw, sensitive nerve. Every touch was exquisite pleasure, sublime pain. Men played my body like a well-tuned instrument. The intensity soared to a crescendo of touch and sound, my soul-deep orgasmic moans the music the men desired.

"'Oh, god!' I climaxed—again—and collapsed against the nearest wall.

"When I could breathe again, I crawled down to the showers; my penis, by this time, limper than my damp towel. As the hot water poured over my spent, satisfied body, I decided it was time to leave. Enough was enough! Besides, what else could I possibly do in my sated, debilitated, de-energized state? On the way to my locker, however, that notion was extinguished by the gentlest of touches.

"The guy who had goosed me was cute—a fuzzy bear with a warm smile and twinkling button eyes—sort of like Dean of Students Werner!" Stuyvesant pointed to the Dean in the front row and the crowd applauded when he waved. Another theatrical pause stretched as Stuyvesant refilled his glass.

"The teddy bear brushed up behind me, slipping his hand under my towel, and squeezed my butt. 'My name is Mike. If you're not going my way, I hope you'll change your mind.' Who could refuse such a gallant invitation?

"Neither of us felt up to any wild acrobatics. Mike had just flown home from a week of gambling in Atlantic City. He'd checked into the club to relax in the steam room before heading to his apartment. But Mike enjoyed licking me, lapping all over my body with his tongue. And he introduced me to my first sex toys—cock rings and poppers!

"As fatigued as I was, my cock reacted promptly to the tight leather strap. And poppers? Woo-hoo! These were the real thing—prescription-grade amyl nitrate—designed for heart patients. I quickly discovered that poppers were a blast—a quick, heady blood-pressure trip, a drop, a surge, a rush—coupled with a hot, heavy whistling electric tornado to my crotch.

"'Yeeeow!' I screamed. I'd never felt anything so powerfully arousing. I responded with a willing erection. Mike gave me another hit. Now knowing what to expect, I inhaled more deeply, holding the vapors for a longer time. When my head was about to blast away from my shoulders and the temperature of my crotch had reached a boiling point, Mike slid two spit-slick fingers up my ass and pressed the hard bulb of my prostate as he deep-throated my cock. The heat of my climax seared my now very tender urethra, and I knew I'd be sore for days. I left Mike dozing on his bed and limped back to the showers, this time actually ready to depart."

Stuyvesant returned to the podium, replacing the microphone. He paused, hands in pockets, and gazed at the top of the lectern as if looking back into that time.

"On the train heading back up to Evanston, I knew—really, truly knew—who I was, who I wanted to be sexually. I wished I could shout my excitement to the hundreds of commuters in the rush-hour crush.

"I had acknowledged to myself, perhaps honestly for the first time, that I preferred men, favored male bodies, craved man sex. I had no doubt about it. There was now no turning back; I wanted only to go farther forward, all the way into this new, exciting world. There could be absolutely no other way! My day at the baths was over, but the course of my life had been changed.

"We had been studying Whitman in my American lit seminar and, as I rattled north watching evening advance across Lake Michigan, a line from 'Out of the Cradle Endlessly Rocking' whispered to me: 'Now in a moment I know what I am for, I awake.'

"I'd been, as it were, reborn. I would never, ever, be the same again."

RELATIONSHIPS

Michael Bracken

My neighborhood had once been home to several warehouses and manufacturing companies, but had been gentrified. Among the first businesses to convert a warehouse into something else was a bathhouse, identifiable to those in the know only because the address was 69 Long Avenue, located at one end of a stub of a street that only stretched for a few blocks and had at the other end a new Starbucks and two art galleries. I'm certain the owners of 69 were aware of the implications of the address well before they purchased and converted the building.

I lived in a loft apartment three stories above the Starbucks, within easy walking distance of the bathhouse in one direction and public transportation in the other. On Long Avenue, and within a several block area surrounding the street, were bistros, galleries, antique stores, funky little clothing shops and my bookstore, a specialty shop not yet in danger from electronic publishing because I specialized in finding out-of-print mystery, science fiction, and sleazecore novels for collectors willing to pay my prices.

Much like many of the neighborhood's other business owners, my interest in the area had been piqued by my 69 membership, and for several years before I joined the neighborhood, I had watched it transform from a collection of abandoned buildings housing an equal number of rats and pigeons to a place where people lived and worked.

Because 69 had been the catalyst that began the transformation, over the years the neighborhood had attracted a certain type of resident, and each day I found myself interacting with a veritable cornucopia of people representing every gender and sexual orientation imaginable in a live-and-let-live environment I'd not experienced elsewhere. It should have been the perfect environment to find the love of my life, but, alas, it was not. A bookworm at heart, I was a failure at relationships. They never lasted long and often ended bitterly when my beau-of-the-month realized I was far more interested in life between the covers of a book than in anything he had to say.

Yet I retained my sexual urges. I still desired the feel of a young man's naked body pressed against mine in carnal congress, so I maintained membership at 69 and visited whenever desire overwhelmed me. Though I might occasionally recognize some of the other members while parading around in nothing but a towel and flip-flops, we often acted as strangers within the confines of 69's sultry, two-story establishment and, more often than not, the usually closeted and sometimes bisexual men I hooked up with came from out of town or from the suburbs.

I had spent the day tracking down copies of two Orrie Hitt sleazecore novels and a trio of Vin Packer's lesbian novels, work I had thrown myself into the day after being dumped by yet another potential paramour, and I had been left sexually unsatisfied by the loss. After treating myself to a light dinner and a glass of wine at a bistro around the corner from my bookstore, I decided a trip to 69—though not a person, my relationship to it was the longest I'd had with anyone or anything—was in order.

Open twenty-four hours a day, seven days a week, 69 is accessible through an electronically dead-bolted solid steel door—a remnant of the days when patron safety was of paramount concern—with the bathhouse's two-digit address typographically enhanced to cover the entire door. I leaned into the bell, waited while the camera above the door caught my image, and then entered after being buzzed in.

I approached the lobby desk and presented my identification to an impeccably dressed young man I found particularly appealing but dared not proposition because bathhouse policy forbade guests and staff from carnal interaction. After he confirmed my membership and I paid for an eight-hour room rental, the young man buzzed me through to the bathhouse proper where an unfamiliar man with the battered face and cauliflower ear of someone who had once worked as a punching bag in a boxing gym handed me a white towel, a pair of blue flip-flops, and my room key suspended from an elastic band.

The two floors of 69 are a dimly lit maze with no direct path from here to there anywhere in the building, with several steam baths, Jacuzzi tubs, dry saunas and a swimming pool. Various rooms had been designed and decorated to represent places where once unsafe assignations could be accommodated safely, from truck-stop glory holes to airport restrooms where would-be senators could slide their feet under the stalls, to a jail cell with padded bars where willing participants could act out prison fantasies, to the balcony seating of a pornographic movie house where explicit movies played nonstop. Light snacks and nonalcoholic drinks were available for purchase as were a variety of sex toys and toiletries, none of which I needed that evening.

Lockers were grouped near the front of the first floor, but private rooms were located on the second floor, and I made my way upstairs past life-size posters of handsome, naked men to the room I had rented. I used my key and pushed open the door, finding a simply decorated room painted a soothing pale blue, with a locker that opened with the same key as the door, a single bed consisting of a vinyl mattress on a wooden frame, and a nightstand next to the bed with a trio of condoms and a small, unopened tube of lube in a wicker basket atop it.

I stripped off my clothes and secured them in the locker. Then I wrapped the towel around my waist, slipped the room key's elastic band around my wrist and hooked a small pill container to the elastic band. After adjusting my glasses, I headed to the sauna.

Except in private areas, 69 discouraged complete nudity, and with everyone wearing the same towel and little else for demarcation of status, we became equals in every way except physical attributes, and men who might not approach one another in the outside world had no qualms about doing so within the confines of the bathhouse.

And so, on my way to the sauna downstairs, other men touched me, some tentatively and others aggressively. Not yet in the mood for companionship, I shook my head at the tentative gropers and pushed away the hands of the aggressive gropers. Once inside the sauna room, where a dozen men had already gathered, I found an open space on the bench, unwrapped my towel so that I was sitting on it nude, and relaxed. Though I let my gaze wander, comparing and contrasting the other men—from the doughy, overweight man in the corner to the muscular hunk of man meat at the end of the bench, their cocks equally diverse in size and shape and their personal grooming habits, or lack of them, on display—the sauna was not a place to hook up, and we all sat in silence, absorbed in our own thoughts. I felt good about my appearance, especially for my age, with only a touch of gray showing at my temples and elsewhere, and the few extra pounds clinging to my waist that easily disappeared when I dressed.

Every few minutes the population of the sauna changed, with men exiting and others entering in no discernable pattern. By the time I felt completely relaxed, no one in the sauna had been there when I arrived. I again wrapped the towel around my waist, exited the sauna and stepped down the hall to the shower, a replica of the showers in a high school gym locker room where men felt free to approach one another. I had the showers to myself, so I took a quick, ice-cold rinse, exchanged my now-wet towel for a clean one and returned the way I had come.

It's disconcerting to have reached an age where Viagra is my only sure path to an erection, but at least I still have my hair, and I actually look good wearing the gold-framed bifocals prescribed to me only a few years earlier to combat increasing nearsightedness. I purchased a bottle of water at the concession stand, downed a Viagra from the pill container I'd attached to my wristband and walked upstairs to my rented room. Leaving the door open, I shed the towel and lay faceup on the single bed, indicating that I was interested in fellatio. There I waited, wondering which I would have first, company or an erection.

One might call it a tie. My cock was partially erect when an attractive blond in his early thirties filled the open doorway and examined me for a moment.

"I saw you in the sauna," he said, "and I liked what I saw. Mind if I join you?"

After I told him I didn't mind, he crossed the room and sat on the side of the bed, next to me. He placed one hand on my leg, his fingers tickling the inside of my thigh. Between his touch and the Viagra coursing through my veins, my cock finished rising to its full stature, seeming all that much bigger because I kept my pubic region closely trimmed.

The blond slid his hand along my leg until he cupped my heavy ball sac, but he did not touch my cock. He kneaded my balls as if weighing and judging them, and he stroked my perineum with the tip of his middle finger. I hadn't noticed it when he'd entered my room, but he'd brought his own lube with him and he stopped massaging my balls just long enough to squeeze a dollop into his palms. He coated my cock shaft with the lube and then returned to massaging my balls and stroking my perineum.

He bent forward and took the head of my cock in his mouth, licked away the drop of precum that had oozed out of the tip while he'd coated my cock with lube and then lowered his face until he had easily taken my entire length into his oral cavity. The blond pulled his face upward until just my cockhead remained between his lips, and then he did it again.

I had just closed my eyes, enjoying the warm, wet sensation of the young blond's mouth on my cock, when a sound from the doorway caught my attention. I opened my eyes to see a dark-haired man standing in the open doorway watching, his towel tented. He appeared to be older than the blond giving me fellatio but was still a good bit younger than me.

"Mind if I watch?" he asked.

When I shook my head, he unfastened the towel, slung it around his shoulders and took his erect cock in his fist. As the blond continued fellating me, the dark-haired man in the doorway jerked off.

The blond's head rose and fell, and he continued massaging my balls. As lube slid from my balls onto my perineum and down my asscrack to soak the sheet beneath me, the blond's head moved faster and faster. Soon I was thrusting my hips upward, my groin meeting each of his face's descents.

The dark-haired man in the doorway came with a grunt, shooting a thin stream of cum halfway across the room, and I knew I was also about to come when my ball sac tightened and my cock stiffened. The blond must have sensed it, too, because he pressed one lube-slickened finger against the tight pucker of my asshole and slid it deep inside me, pressing my prostate.

I couldn't stop myself. I closed my eyes, thrust upward one last time and came, firing wad after thick wad of warm cum against the back of the blond's throat. He eagerly swallowed every drop, not letting the tiniest bit escape from between his lips.

By the time my cock stopped throbbing in the blond's mouth and I finally opened my eyes, the dark-haired man had abandoned the doorway. When the blond was certain I had finished, he removed his finger from my ass and released his oral grip on my rapidly deflating cock.

He sat upright and stared down into my eyes.

I said, "I haven't seen you here before."

"This is my first time," he said. "I just moved into the neighborhood."

"If I see you here again—" I didn't finish my sentence.

"Of course."

He patted my thigh, then stood and adjusted his towel. On his way out, he closed the door so that I would not be disturbed during postorgasm recovery.

I lay in the bed for half an hour before I finally rose. Then I used my towel to wipe the lube from my cock, crotch and asscrack before I opened the locker and retrieved my clothes.

After I dressed, I pocketed the unused condoms and lube, and left 69 with time remaining on my eight-hour room rental, satiated and thankfully without any obligation for postcoital relationship-status conversation. I returned to my loft apartment, tucked myself into bed alone and promised myself I would not attempt another relationship when satisfactory anonymous sex was available twenty-four hours a day a mere three blocks from home.

It was a lie I only believed until I met the new blond Starbucks barista the next morning on my way to my bookstore. The milk foam head he put on my Grande latte was just as impressive as the head he'd given me the night before.

The blond winked as he handed me the latte.

I thought maybe I should try one more time for a lasting relationship. I asked, "Do you like old books?"

SAUNSATIONAL

Landon Dixon

I was sitting by myself in the sauna. The heat was turned up high, the steam thick and wet. I was wearing just a white towel around my slim hips, and I had a hand burrowed down in the towel, softly, languidly stroking my hard, pulsating cock. A strenuous late-night session on the weights had left me feeling drained and fulfilled, glowing and aroused.

The door popped open and a man intruded on my reverie.

I jerked my hand out of the towel and flung it up to my red hair. "H-hi," I said, watching the man step up onto the third tier of cedar benches opposite me.

"Hi, yourself," he responded, his voice rich and deep. He leaned back against the cedar-panelled wall and let out a sigh. "Feels good, huh?"

"Yeah...sure does."

He was twice my young age, built twice as big. His huge, black muscular upper body mushroomed up out of the skimpy tight towel. Dark, thick-muscled legs poured out from the bottom. He was shaved smooth all over like a bodybuilder, with pumped up pecs, arms and thighs. His ebony skin gleamed with perspiration.

I felt my cock stiffen under my towel.

"Haven't seen you around before," he rumbled, looking at me.

"No! This is my first time." And I wasn't just talking about working out at the gym.

"You'll like it. Good people here. I come all the time." He grinned, teeth flashing white. "Mind if I ditch the towel?" His brown eyes twinkled through the mist.

I gulped, staring at his big, beautiful, glistening body and high-planed, handsome face. "Um, no…not at all. Go right—"

He arched his butt off the bench and pulled off the towel. His cock was large and thick, a mahogany log even soft. I licked my parched lips, feeling my cock surge, my body swell with heat.

I felt heavy, heady, like I was in a trance; the sight of that naked, muscle-bound hunk made me dizzy with lust. Never had I been in the presence of such overpowering masculinity.

"Ah, that's the stuff," he growled, shifting around on the bench, his dick hanging between his legs. "Name's Troy, by the way." He offered his hand.

I was too far away to accept his greeting. I couldn't connect with the man without getting up and going over. I *had* to connect. I got up and went over, drawn like gravity, compelled.

I stumbled down my tier and staggered up his. I grabbed my towel as it started to slip from my waist. I shook his hand. "Cody!" I said. He pulled me up onto his bench. I plopped down next to him, thin and white and young, a boy alongside this god.

"Nice to meet you, Cody." He pointed at my left pec. "Looks like you got some development going on there."

I jerked, goose bumps burning across my sallow chest at the touch of the he-man. "Th-thanks!"

He closed his eyes and leaned his head back against the wall, spreading his legs wider apart. His huge shoulder brushed up against mine. "You don't look so bad yourself," I said. "Can I feel it?" The last set of words spilled out of my mouth along with a string of saliva.

Troy opened his eyes and smiled at me. "Sure. Go to town." He flexed his pecs, making the dark mounds with the even darker tips dance right before my staring green eyes.

"I'm just, you know...I'd, uh, like to get as big as you...one day. So—"

He pulled my left hand off of the wood and planted it on the muscle—his right pec. I grinned, giddy, feeling the clenched mass pop under my palm. I spread my fingers out over his nipple. I brushed my fingers across his chest.

Troy grunted and closed his eyes again, shifted his feet, setting his hanging cock in motion.

I stared down at his cock. It started to thicken. I clutched his pec, strummed the ripe, rigid nipple, hardly believing what was happening. His cock was definitely rising, engorging!

I swallowed hard, and my throat cracked dry despite the 110 percent humidity. I shifted around and threw my right hand onto Troy's left pec, gripping that mass of muscle. "Y-yeah, you really got it going, all right!" I garbled, groping the man's pecs, gazing at his cock that was sticking out from his hips.

"Take a taste, if you want," he said.

There was no doubting his intent. My face flushed red as my hair. It was happening—I was pushing my head forward, tasting the hard, rubbery texture of his nipple.

We both jerked with impact.

I anxiously swirled my tongue around Troy's dark nipple,

making it shine and swell even further as I looked up into Troy's liquid-brown eyes. He smiled, popping his pec under my tongue. I roped my lips over the straining bud. I sealed them around his nipple and sucked.

A tremor ran through his big body. I nursed like a hungry infant, sucking hard and tight on the man's nipple, squeezing his pecs. I yanked my head back, plunged it over, engulfing and consuming his other equally flared nipple and tugging on it.

I thought I'd melt. My face and body were on fire. Troy cupped the back of my head with a huge hand and pulled me back, gazing into my glassy eyes. "How 'bout helping me out with that new development you created?" His eyes rolled downward.

My orbs followed, down his rock-ribbed stomach to his granite-hard cock. His cock was hard, twelve inches of manhood. "Yes, please!"

He helped me head down. I pulled my fingers off of his chest and laced them around his cock, gripping his dick top and bottom like I'd been charming snakes all my sexual life.

"Yeah!" Troy grunted, thrusting his dong upward between my damp little palms. It passionately throbbed in my hands.

I bent over the enormous erection, staring into the blue-black bloated cap, riding my hands up and down. I was stroking, pumping the man's cock, righteously feeling the thick, pulsating, vein-ribboned length of dark meat. It was incredible, wickedly intimate. My knuckles blazed white on the beating black dong.

Troy pushed my head farther down. My lips kissed up against his gaping slit. I kissed and licked it, opened my mouth up wide and took his knob right inside.

I was as shocked as anyone.

"That's the stuff!" Troy groaned, shooting more massive cock into my mouth.

I couldn't see, couldn't think clearly, the steam and lust clouding my eyes and head like the man's dick was crowding my mouth. I bent my neck down at his urging, inhaling more of his pipe. It pulsed powerfully in my mouth, thundering like the blood in my ears, the beefy hood bumping up against the back of my throat. My lips stretched obscenely, my face crammed with cock, my own prick a steel rod tenting my towel.

"Suck it!" Troy growled in a deep bass.

I sucked his huge member, vacuuming tight and drooling, Troy helping me bob my head up and down. I only gagged a little, pulling hard on his meat with my mouth. My nostrils flared, sweat poured off my forehead and down onto Troy's big balls. His hips picked up the pace, pumping his cock into me so I could go deeper, more depraved.

"How 'bout I fuck you? Workout that ass of yours?"

A tingle shot through my chute. I'd never been fucked by a man before, except in innumerable fantasies, of course. I'd never sucked a man's cock or tasted his cum before, either; but that's exactly, amazingly what I was doing—tasting a spurt of salty precum from the dong I was excitedly sucking.

Troy pulled my head up. His cock slid out of my mouth, leaving me gapingly empty. It stood tall between his thighs, spit-slickened and leaking precum thanks to yours truly. Troy helped swing me around, so that I ended up in his lap, sitting astride his muscular thighs in front of his jutting hammer.

My towel was lost in the erotic transfer. My own cock pronged up straight and hard and throbbing pink, right next to Troy's deep-dark dong. He gripped the pair together in his big, warm hand and pumped.

I almost shot up into the air with the sensual impact. But I managed to grab on to Troy's cinder-block shoulders just in time. I stared dazedly into his brown eyes, feeling every torrid inch of his erection pinned against my erection, our cocks burning together, melding with the pump of his hand. It was the most exquisite sensation I'd ever experienced—up to that point.

"Nice pubic muscle," Troy breathed in my face.

Then he kissed me, his plush lips splashing into mine, his brilliant tongue shooting into my open mouth. I feebly tried to tongue him back, but his thick, swirling, wet licker easily overpowered mine. So I just hung on and let him thrash around inside my mouth, as he churned our cocks together faster and faster.

"Troy! I'm going to...I'm going to...!" I gasped, the superheated sexual situation too much for a rank amateur like myself. The guy had too much experience, too much equipment for me to compete at his level.

He immediately snapped his tongue out of my mouth and whipped his hand off our pressed cocks. "Not yet, Cody! I've got to work out that cute little ass of yours yet, remember?"

A small bottle of lube magically appeared. I didn't even think it was necessary with all of the sweat and steam, but Troy knew best, knew just how big he was, and would feel. I watched him grease his nightstick. Then he hooked an arm around my waist and lifted me up and slid a blunt finger in between my quivering white buttcheeks, rubbed my frightened starfish slick.

"Ready?" he asked.

My mouth opened and closed like I was about to be gaffed.

Troy gripped his cock, pushed the cap up between my cheeks and against my pucker. I hung suspended on the beefy tip of his spear, not breathing. Then my butt ring buckled under the tremendous pressure, flowered. Troy's hood squished into my chute, stretching my anus.

I groaned, shaking wildly. He gripped my thin waist with both of his big hands and pressed me down onto his black spike.

Shaft glided into my ass, bloating it, stuffing me, inches and inches of thick cock.

My rippling bum touched down on his clenched thighs. His cock was buried up my ass. It felt like that dong would come right out my throat it was cramming me so full. The sensations were strange and wicked and wonderful. I was electrified like never before with that cable coursing up my butt, making me blaze.

Troy painted my parted lips with his tongue, slowly lifting me up and bringing me down on his pile driver. I clung to his shoulders, barely able to breathe, to comprehend, a mass of flaming, raw, nervy joy. He thrust his hips in rhythm to his lifting, churning my chute with his cock.

My internal temperature raged like an inferno, the smooth pumping action incendiary. My own cock bounced right along, stiff as a frozen rope in that sexual steam bath.

Troy moved faster, stroking long and hard into my anus. I blinked for the first time, flung a sheet of sweat off my face with a toss of my head. I could see clearly now, feel everything. A man was fucking my virgin ass; he'd popped my anal cherry and now was drilling me deep as a cock could go. I helped him, bouncing up and down in his lap, riding his thrusting cock.

He grinned; his teeth gritted together, face shining with perspiration, fierce with lust. I kissed him, tongued sweat off his upper lip and chin, impaling myself on his meat.

He thrust faster. A man fucking another man up the ass is the most natural and beautiful workout there is. The wooden bench creaked and our tightened flesh cracked together, our breath coming in gasps.

"Fuck, Cody! I'm gonna—"

"Me, too!"

He hammered up my chute in a frenzy, tossing me into the

air. My wildly flapping cock erupted; spouting sizzling semen all over Troy's clenched pecs and abs. I cried with pure bliss, riding the man's ramrod as he howled and bucked, blasted steaming sperm up my butt.

I was coming; a man was coming inside me, my wildest dreams coming true. It went on and on, my cock spurting forever, his cock shooting me full of an ecstasy I'd never before known existed.

I probably lost ten pounds off my slender frame in that cauldron of a sauna, along with my innocence. And then I almost lost my mind, when, half an hour later, I saw Troy leaving the gym with a *woman*, whom he introduced as his wife.

"Cody and I are workout buddies, Rachel," he explained to the statuesque redhead. Then he grinned at me. "Same time, same place on Wednesday...buddy?"

My head bobbed up and down like it had in the gorgeous guy's lap.

I couldn't wait for another sauna session with Troy, so he could develop me further as a man.

ACROSS THE BAY

T. R. Verten

By day he works in an office. He wears pin-striped suits, tucks his shirts in, courts clients, sits in on conference calls, and is bored beyond belief. Felipe Nascimento has a great job, a condo and a stellar, shining portfolio. Felipe is an asset to the institution and the most competent junior hire, by far. He will probably be promoted soon, and with that will come a larger expense account and better suits and bigger steaks, and he will, by day and on work nights, be on the top of his game, in charge, in control and calling the shots.

But not on Friday nights.

Mondays through Thursdays he goes to the gym before work and goes out with donors for lunches and attends charity functions in the evenings. He DVRs television, reads the paper, feeds his gray-haired Scottish fold cat and is in control of every single aspect of his life.

Felipe could use a little less control, on occasion.

That is why on Fridays he goes home—stopping off at a bar

with his coworkers for a happy-hour drink or three—and then watches television while stretching, on the floor, in front of the screen. He sits cross-legged in sweatpants, to open up his hips, and then he does pigeon pose, twice on each side. When he is limber and loose he will have a glass or two of wine, if he feels fancy, and vodka if he is agitated, and then he takes a cab to the East Bay where he's able to lose control for a couple of hours, and in those hours of the week, he feels the most alive of all.

Amazing, he thinks, what goes on in secret, behind blacked-out doors and paint-covered windows. So much of life is lived publicly these days, everyone checking in here and there, updating, liking, tweeting, exclaiming, and declaiming—*Here I am! look at me!* But he does not enable geo-targeting on his phone, on Friday nights: no texts, no push notifications, no automatic autocorrect of *Here I am, look at me.*

The taxi will pull up in front of a long, low concrete building.

Inside, once he flashes his card and puts his things in a locker, takes a shower and ties a towel around his waist, he will go, water streaming down the back of his neck from his still-wet hair, into the main room, which is nearly as hot as the rain forest. The noises are different than the forest, but the quiet drip of water is pretty much the same. Felipe has only been in the Amazon once, but the memory of lush wetness, stinky damp, a pervasive odor of rot—that is the same feeling he gets, initially, when he walks into this room, late Friday night, when he is loose and the crowd is attentive.

Felipe lives his life in the open, in the daytime, every night except for Fridays.

On Fridays he is excited to be watched.

Felipe likes the attention; he is, after all, a closet narcissist.

Though he is not closeted on the job, he likes to keep his private life just that: private. He does not ask what Amy in marketing gets up to online (though he suspects she reads gay vampire porn) or what Dylan in fundraising does (amateur lesbian vids on Redtube, he's sure of it), or what Larry their vice president likes to do (too gross to even contemplate)—so he wants, obviously, to keep this all under wraps.

Were anyone in his real life, his regular life, to know about his Friday nights, he could say with certainty that they would speculate: that he has parental issues, low self-esteem, bad self-image, hang-ups, problems, an eating disorder, an abusive childhood, a gaping hole, a loss of innocence, a broken heart.

Felipe does not agree.

Felipe just likes to get fucked, with no goddamned complications.

One partner is good, many partners even better. Many with many more onlookers are probably the best of all.

It is humid and crowded, smoggy and dimly lit. He makes a loop, drinks some water, checks out his options. There is a hot guy with stubble, eyes that burn blue even in the low light, and freckles on his shoulders. Nice mouth, amazing fingers, and hung like a fucking horse. Felipe goes to stand four or so feet away from this man, whose eyes flick over and appraise him. He stands up a little straighter, arches his back out, eyes focused straight ahead on three guys—two white and one black—making out. He props one foot up against the tile wall and presses his palms against it, watching.

The man comes over and leans up into Felipe's space, his hand resting above the top of Felipe's head. Felipe does not look away, but he bites his lip and sucks it into his mouth when the man unknots his towel and lets it fall onto the slippery floor. He has mean fingers and a good mouth, and he rubs his stubbly cheek along Felipe's inner thighs, drawing up hot red bumps. He puts one hand on either hip and puts his lips around him, and that—yeah, he watches that like crazy, his hips twitching forward until he is about to come, and he looks down and shakes his head no, and the stranger kisses the tip of his cock, and stands back up.

There is a press of watching bodies on either side of him, but they back up when Felipe turns around and pushes his ass out, spreads his legs, hands above his head like he's about to be frisked. The man kisses Felipe's neck, licks the fresh sweat dripping down it and breathes heavy in his ear. He has wet fingers and he is wriggling them into Felipe's ass, curling them and making his cock twitch, reflexively. The man fingers him for what feels like a long time, and his mouth grows dry and his stomach feels queasy, sick with deferred release. He wants to get off and yet wants more fingers—three and then four, maybe five, all five, splitting him open for everyone to see, his ass taking it, so hungry, so willing—

"Unnngh," he groans, into the cradle of his hands.

From over his shoulder, he hears one man laugh, and then one say, "You need to fill that fucking hole, man," and someone else says, "Fuck, that's hot," and he does not feel ashamed; he feels gorgeous, amazing, exonerated—

"Yeah?" says the guy with the better part of his hand in Felipe's ass, "You want that?"

"Fuck me," Felipe grits out. "Know you want to."

The loss of pressure stings when the man pulls his fingers out, and then he can feel the hot tip of his dick pressing, lingering there. He eases Felipe back by the hip and nudges in, just the head, so hot, so fucking delicious and slick and Felipe says, "Come on, man, do it fucking *right*," and the guy laughs, kind of mean, and says, "Take my cock then, I'll fill you all up, you pushy little shit," and he shifts his hips right and then left and then he is being filled, so powerfully and exquisitely that he lets out a hollow squeal and loses the power of speech, pretty much entirely.

The man fucks him hard, a hand on the back of his neck and one on his hip, guiding him, steering him, using him. Felipe loves this moment, lives for it, when he can feel a hard cock in his ass and a dozen pairs of eyes on him, and he is the focus of everyone's attention and soon to be a convenient come receptacle.

That is the bit that sends him over, and he manages to grunt out, "Pull out, pull out," and the guy does, pulling off the condom and shooting his load all over Felipe's ass. It trickles down his thighs as he drops a hand down to tug on his cock, and the man cups his balls with one hand, slips his fingers into Felipe's ass, still wet with lube from before, and Felipe slaps his hand against the dripping tile wall and shudders out, "Fuck, fuck, yeah."

After, he has to catch his breath. The man kisses him on the mouth and smiles and says, "Thank you," and Felipe says, "No problem," and then he takes a shower and gets a cab back to his place.

And he does not ever once feel bad about this.

Why the hell should he?

Two weeks in a row he goes back there. One encounter is unsatisfactory (the dreaded micro-penis) and the other was rote. It droned on for far too long, the guy sawing his hips back and forth and grunting until Felipe wanted to shout *Fucking come already, asshole.* On Saturday he goes to the gym and then out to a party, one with college people, not one for work, and his girlfriends try to make him talk to the bartender.

"He has such incredible triceps," Julia says, sucking down

the last of her mojito with a skinny double straw. "Hit that for all of us, Felipe, baby."

He laughs, because it is funny, and because it is true.

If he wanted, he could have hooked up with that bartender, who has on a tight black T-shirt creeping up along the biceps to reveal a bunch of tattoos. Nice triceps, indeed.

It is just before midnight on the following Friday when he drives down, stone-cold sober. He goes back to that same bar and checks out a different bartender, who is twinky and sort of shrimpy, and does fuck-all for Felipe's libido.

Whether by luck or coincidence the guy that he screwed three weeks ago is there when he walks into the steamy room, his flip-flops squelching across the wet tile. He is leaning back against a wall, his jaw regal, his dick hard, and Felipe blinks to clear his head. He takes a breath that catches in his chest and picks his way across the room. The man notices him when he is about six feet away, and fixes Felipe with a look that is part leer and part warning.

The last few feet seem to take forever.

They greet each other like old lovers, a touch of familiarity in the way the other man's hand circles Felipe's head, fingers threading through his hair to tug him into a filthy kiss. Felipe feels cold on the back of his neck, even though the room is hot with steam. He buries his head in the man's chest, rubbing his face against his shoulders, waiting to be told what to do next. Over his own deep inhales the man whispers, "Do you want to put your mouth on me, baby?" and Felipe nods, furiously.

"Get on your knees then," he says, pushing Felipe away and down.

The tile is slippery and it hurts, because his knees are bony and uncushioned. He looks around to see if anyone is watching and then takes his towel off, folding it over twice like a yoga mat.

And then he is totally bare in front of two-dozen strangers, that firm hand pulling roughly on the back of his head and shoving him forward so that he topples and overbalances for a moment. He works his way back up with his nose along the man's thigh, and then his crotch, inhaling deeply the smell of his cock, and the man chuckles, asking, "Does that smell good?"

Felipe looks up and nods, feeling a comforting thumb rub under his ear and the man's blue eyes are dark with strain and he says, "Tastes even better," and Felipe whimpers under his breath as the towel is stripped away and there is a hard cock in his face. He opens his mouth without even being told, rising up on his knees to get the angle right, and fuck, it's so good. Felipe sucks gently on the head, swirls his tongue and the moans he is making are not just for show; he is so hard, his ass exposed, his cock bobbing uselessly against his stomach as the man grabs either side of his face and forces him up and down on his cock.

"Mmmmph," Felipe chokes, six separate times when his gag reflex is triggered. The man pulls away each time and lets Felipe catch his breath, gasping, until he falls back upon the cock in his face, hungrily. When the man comes, Felipe swallows. Some of it spills out the sides, and he uses his finger to clean himself up, licking it lewdly.

"Jesus," the man says. "You'll eat anything, won't you?"

Felipe is pleased with himself, even more pleased when the man pulls him into a backward embrace so that he is facing the room, a fair portion of which is paying attention, and wraps a hand around his poor neglected hard-on and uses the other hand to manipulate his hips.

"Fuck my fist, there you go. I can feel your cock pulsating in my hand. You feel that? You want to come, let everyone see you shoot your load all over the place, baby, is that what you want? Yeah, you like that, don't you, don't you...?"

Felipe's hips are twitching forward of their own accord and he is twisting from side to side, trying to find the right angle to get off, but when he gets close the man pulls his hand away or eases up his grip, and Felipe feels his orgasm retreat in a hazy rush, over and over again, so that by the time he is finally allowed to come, his dick is sore and purple with rough stroking. It is still chafed the next day, and he has to buy salve and wear his softest pair of underwear.

Felipe travels to the DC offices the following week and then the weekend after that he visits his family in Boca—breakfast with his mother, pool time, lunch at the club with relatives. He finds that the distance helps. When his mother cannot drop by unexpectedly, when he does not have to do the call-and-response of questions over salmon and pea puree. It is a relief to be back in San Francisco, the air thirty degrees cooler, the fog a welcome change from humid smog. Friends take him dancing the next night and he gets far too drunk. They end up in an overpriced diner adjacent to North Beach: Felipe orders cheese fries he does not touch and a vanilla milkshake, which he drinks greedily.

He and Julia split a taxi after that, and he contemplates telling it to go over the bridge, but he's worn out. The milkshake makes him burp. At home, in his condo, he strips off all his sweaty clothes and stands under the shower for a long time, letting the hot water cascade off his face and into his open mouth. Dripping from his calves onto the marble tile, he wraps a towel around his waist and then dries his hair with another.

The hot water has knocked some of the evening's funk off of him, and he feels lighter now that he is clean. He takes out his iPad and dicks around on the Internet for a while, which includes a bleary scroll through some pornography, which kind of fills his need for cock, and he jerks off, resting on his side and fucking into his hand before leaning back to come on his stomach. He uses the towel to clean himself off and puts it in the laundry hamper.

It is three a.m. before he falls into a dreamless sleep.

The next week is full of follow-up calls from the meeting of a week prior. Everyone in the DC office seems solid, though some of them drone on for far too long during conference calls. He puts on a headset and plays Tetris on his phone when they start talking to one another, animatedly. Come Friday, he ducks out of work early and goes to a yoga class. On the way back to his place he stops for sushi, which he eats from a china plate in front of the television.

Julia texts: *do u want to hit up arcade with us? sarah and lucy are coming.*

He texts back: *sry maybe another time*

hot date?

fuck you

lol we tried once

yr never gonna let me live that down

it'll make a great story for our children

not that again

u owe me sperm

gross

u love it

brunch sun?

totally

<3

xx

He stretches his inner thighs by sitting wide-legged in front of the television, on the floor, and then he gets up, pulls on a fleece jacket and shoves his feet into gym shoes, and heads out. He has brought just enough cash for a taxi there and back, because he does not want to have anything else on him: no phone, no car keys, no wallet. Nothing, save a thin roll of twenties and a couple of breath mints.

The ride is slow because of traffic. Without his phone he has nothing to do but stare out the window and think, but not really think. It is more akin to fantasizing—not, precisely, "getting in the mood," because there is a part of Felipe that is always pretty much in the mood. Of course he has no plans to start sucking off the COO (though he is sexy, in a silver fox sort of a way) or hook up with tons of randoms when he goes out with his girlfriends, but when he goes out like this, on his own, he knows what he wants to happen.

Felipe has used the Internet, mobile technology, geotargeting—all those things, to locate and be located—*Look at me! Here I am!*—but only for pictures of pectoral muscles reflected in bathroom mirrors, abdomens, cock shots. It's the same with ads, missed connections and personals on the Internet. Conditions of anonymity are part of it, being watched is certainly another. Felipe prefers to venture out on his own, without company either human or technological. Simply to feel—to feel and most of all to be felt. Felipe smiles a little in the reflection of the back window. His own face smiles back. When they arrive at the low-slung stucco building, Felipe thanks the driver and tips him generously.

Inside it is humid, with a smell not unlike a school gym, which borders on disgusting but touches something inside him, a thing both primal and shockingly intimate—memories of attraction, flashes of other boys changing, the smell of the locker room after a soccer game, jerking off into one mismatched kneesock all through his sophomore year, which he washed alone, in the bathroom sink, twice a month. Boys are gross, Felipe knows, filthy and crusty, their bodies racing courses of hormones and imagination, with only thoughts of tits (most boys) and dick (him) pulsating through their minds and crotches.

Grown men are really no different, he thinks, as he walks into the main area, letting his eyes adjust to the darkness. The recovery time may be longer and the interval between orgasms lasts upwards of a week, but men like to get off, just like boys do, whether they do it by jerking off in front of a computer screen or in the shower, or, as Felipe is watching several other strangers do, in a room where action is taking place.

There is a wooden bench of the kind you find in mid-priced gyms over to one side. People are clustered around it, so Felipe goes to stand behind the huddled group. He is pretty tall, close to six feet, and even though there are people in front he can see okay. It is the man from a few weeks ago, who fucked him a month ago against the wall not twelve feet away, only this time he is fucking another guy, tan like Felipe, but much more buff, with standard-issue star tattoos on his arms and a tribal design on his left calf.

Felipe can see his calf the most clearly of all, as the other man's fingers splay wide and push it back farther, so that the guy on the bench is being folded over backward, in on himself, his ass lifted up so high that he is being fucked from above, almost, rather than the side or horizontally, and even at this distance Felipe hears heated slapping of skin on skin and a hollow wooden noise as they bang against the bench, moving in tandem.

Of course he is aroused, but he is also oddly jealous of the guy on the bench, though whether he is more jealous of who is fucking him or all the attention he is getting he is not sure. Either way, he puts it out of his mind and watches them finish. Some people clap when it is over. His cock is hard but he feels queasy, so he goes into a cooler room and splashes some cold water on his face.

When he goes back in the huddle has dispersed. He leans against the far wall and then gets fucked against it by a beefy man with a goatee. As he braces himself against the slippery tile and pistons his hips back to drive that cock in as deep as it will go, he turns his head to the side because he feels someone enter his field of vision.

He is watching Felipe from a few feet away, and Felipe's mouth falls open wetly as the man fucking him hits his prostate and his eyes flutter closed, the room going dark.

The last thing he sees is piercing blue eyes.

The last thing he feels is an unwarranted sense of betrayal.

Once he opens his eyes again, after they have both come, he finds that their looker has left.

He gasps and lets himself be kissed before going to shower and take a cab back to his place.

The week seems long, the interval between punctuated moments of excitement excruciating. No plans have been made, nor names exchanged, but Felipe is eager to see his stranger once more. He resolves to get there early, so as not to miss his window of opportunity. When he arrives at the bathhouse, freshly showered and scrubbed shining inside and out, the sun has only just set. It is pretty empty, and he feels stupid, standing in a wet tiled room waiting for a man who has never once promised to meet him. Felipe continues to feel stupid when he does not show up. After an hour-plus of lurking and turning down offers, he leaves.

He is not there the next week.

Or the following week.

Nor the one after that.

So he stops going for a while. Felipe does not usually fixate like this, on one person, and it is kind of pathetic, so he tries to get on with his life. Julia sets him up on a couple of dates with her coworkers, and she talks, too, about her cousin from L.A. that Felipe just *has to meet*, but it doesn't progress beyond that.

He travels back East for Thanksgiving.

In Miami he goes to a seedy bar and gets a blow job from a black boy in a cheap leather jacket. His mouth is wickedly hot and Felipe comes hard down his throat, using the flat of his hand to push his head *down down down* and watch it bob. He does not get fucked like he wants to there, though. He does not get fucked like he wants to for a while, actually.

After New Year's—when he and Julia throw a party at his place, putting heat lamps out on the rooftop deck and catering in tiny portions of American comfort food—he goes back across the bay, and resolves to be less silly. In the shower, he washes his skin until it squeaks and then walks around, through the halls with private rooms off to the sides, through which emanates the occasional slap or groan or cry. Felipe has never been in a private room. He likes to be seen, and that is less likely behind locked doors. And there is fear, as well, of the dangers of intimacy. The exchange of names and fluids. It does not progress beyond the main room because Felipe does not want it to.

Perhaps it is the long absence from this place, but it all seems novel once more.

And the scene unfolding on the bench in front of him is novel, as well.

Usually it is pretty straightforward.

There is, he knows, a whole other scene in the Bay Area, leather and fetishists, bondage and submission and coming on command. Hints of it are always in the air: men will come in and use the public space the way that is happening now. Felipe walks around to the side and peers through the gap left by shoulders to see what is happening. What he sees makes his cock swell and the muscles in his jaw twitch. It is hot, and terrifying, and he cannot tear his eyes away.

A well-muscled guy with dark hair is kneeling, naked, with his upper arms and wrists bound behind his back. He is wearing a perforated leather blindfold and he is sucking the cock of a third man, who is using his hips to get leverage. The one on his knees is being pushed from behind, one hand on his head and one on his upper back shoving him down hard onto the cock in his face. He goes up and down easily, and keeps his mouth tight except when he flinches, which he does every thirty seconds or so because a different man, a fourth man with sinewy forearms and a graying goatee, uses a short leather strap to hit him in different places, like his shoulders and his upper back.

Felipe lets out a long, low whistle under his breath and cranes his head to get a better view. The sub is moaning through his mouthful of cock, and even though he thrashes when he gets hit, he moans even louder each time. No one has ever done such a thing to Felipe, so he does not know how it feels. But it looks amazing, and he is palming himself through his rough towel, watching like everyone else.

"Don't turn around," comes a voice against his ear, as a body slides into place behind him. Felipe gasps when his earlobe is sucked into an anonymous mouth; he groans when a firm hand slides down his front and twists each of his nipples in turn; he gasps when fingers trail along his belly and under his towel; he whimpers when the towel is not taken off but a second hand spider-walks up the back of his thighs and a long finger comes to rest in the crack of his ass.

"Do you think that's hot?" asks the voice.

Felipe nods, eyes fixed forward.

"Mmm," he says, wriggling a second finger into his crack and moving it, "Like to see you like that, sometime," he goes on, and then he kisses his way down Felipe's arched spine to the swell of his ass, nipping each dimple at the base. He tugs Felipe's towel down until it lies in a heap.

The man getting his dick sucked is coming; he is quickly replaced by the one who was doing the hitting. Someone else steps forward to do that. From over his right shoulder, Felipe hears a whistle. Hands part his asscheeks gently, and every inch of his backside is covered with soft kisses, until he is panting and balling his hands into fists.

"Fuck," he mumbles, feeling a tongue press into him as the sub on his knees takes the third cock of the night and starts to suck it, more slowly than before. He must be out of breath, Felipe thinks, especially now that the man he's kneeling in front of is choking him on his dick. There are two hands on his head, and when he lowers down he gags. At one point the man holding his hands pulls him up and lets him catch his breath, red faced.

It is at that moment that the stranger slips a finger into Felipe. He continues to bite the swell of his ass. With those two fingers he fills Felipe with cock, and Felipe keeps watching. With his hands on his upper thighs he ruts back onto the fingers pounding into him. Then that mouth, again, in him and on him and doing everything to him. He waits to come until the third man getting blown expresses his intention to do the same, and the man eating Felipe's ass pulls hard on his hips, and he cups his cock with one hand and comes with shuddery bucks of his hips.

The sub is untethered and helped to stand up. He has marks on his arms from the restraints.

The stranger kisses the back of Felipe's neck and says, "Eyes forward until I'm gone," and for whatever reason, Felipe listens.

When he leaves there is no one outside.

Not until three months have passed does he see him, on his way inside on a Friday night, sitting on a black motorcycle and smoking a cigarette.

Felipe is fully prepared to walk right past him, but the stranger beckons with a finger and Felipe goes over to him, and when he asks, he tells him his name.

MEANWHILE IN THE SAUNA...

Jimi Goninan

Why does it smell like cinnamon in here? Maybe it's a new cleaning product; even so it doesn't seem quite appropriate. God, it's slow in here tonight. Well, at least it's better than the time that I accidentally nodded off in a cubicle and woke to find myself the only gay in the sauna...oops!

Seriously, what the hell am I doing here? It seems like every day it's the same routine. Strip off, pop a breath mint—a practice I wish everyone had the courtesy to follow—then wander 'round in a towel for hours on end in the vain hope of meeting Mr. Right, or at least Mr. Right Now; hopefully even several.

When are they going to fix the tiles on this bench? Someone's going to hurt himself on that jagged edge, especially if he's flouncing around in here naked. A few bumps and bruises are all right, but I much prefer to get them the old-fashioned way, in the throes of passion, rather than due to dodgy maintenance. Although maybe not in quite as embarrassing a way as that nasty black eye I got when I fell off the bench mid-action. Honestly with what they charge you'd think there'd be better upkeep.

Have I always been this cynical and cranky? Dear lord, I sound just like my grand-dad. Although I don't think that I'm ready for retirement just yet.

I spend way too much time in here, although it's good for my skin and I need all the flattering lighting I can get these days. The sparkly lights on the ceiling really are mesmerizing, all pretty and star-like. So relaxing I could just look at them for hours, listening to that soothing, dripping accompaniment.

Ow! Fuck, that stings! Just what I needed...a drop of hot water straight in the eye! I don't even want to think about what heady mix of chemical and biologically infused liquid I just got dosed with. Well, it's probably no worse than anything else I willingly expose myself to in here. Serves me right for daydreaming.

Time for a wander, I think.

Stop feeling sorry for yourself; no one wants to jump you if you're radiating "I hate the world" vibes. Have enough trouble picking up these days without all that.

What did I just tread in? I really hope that isn't what I think it is. Gross! My foot's all greasy and nasty. Man up! It's hardly the worst thing I've encountered lurking on the floors here. Can't people pick up after themselves? No manners these days. Oh, well, nothing a quick trip back to the showers won't fix, besides it's a good excuse to go perve.

Fucking hell, the size of the dick on that one, you'd be feeling him for a week!

Have I slept with him or not? Yes...yes, I have and he was hopeless if memory serves. I mean really, how hard is it? Just because you're endowed doesn't mean that no further effort on your part is required. Honestly, some boys just have no idea what the fuck they're doing; we all have the same basic bits, you shouldn't need a degree to know what to tweak, lick and tug.

Oh, I love this song...

Nothing quite like the delightful soundtrack of grunts, slaps and slurps, but sometimes I do love a good beat.

Although there are boys that definitely need some sort of etiquette guidebook to teach them the appropriate behavior in places like this. Dirty, raunchy sex—YES! Practicing your fantasy drag act—NO! There are just some things that should be left to the privacy of your own home.

Is he even eighteen?

I never looked that young; I swear he's like a baby. God, I hated when the older queens called me that. But it's true, he looks so innocent; the ultimate Boy Scout type. Perhaps not so much the other day, when he was being fucked every which way in the orgy room, with that look of absolute ecstasy in his eyes and wailing like a cat in heat.

Attitude much!

I'm sorry, matey, but we are all here for the same thing, even if you do have abs for days and an ass that just begs to be played with. Fine, ignore me, plenty more roosters in the barn.

God, I sound so old. Good thing I don't actually speak to them, not if I can help it anyway. Although at least I'm a little bit more polite than that one.

It's a nonstop parade of flesh in here, complete with the obligatory judging. Too short, too tall, too old...he really needs to hit the gym/solarium/hairdresser...does he even own a mirror...how dare he even look in my direction? I'm so out of his league!

Well, now, who would I rather be—that tormented and lonely fat kid from school or the unobtainable, overly confident god judging from high? No more crying in the corner for this little pink duck.

Man, he's just delicious. I haven't seen him in here before... ah, damn already taken...by him...seriously? He's so stunning, what's he doing with that troll? I'm so much hotter than him, what's the deal? Twinks with grandpas...daddy issues much? I'm awful...but funny and that's the important thing.

It's so predatory here—the hunt, the chase, the kill. Stalking my prey, through the darkened corridors and over the slick and slippery floors, desperate to add another conquest to my *slutastically* long list.

Who am I kidding? I love it...when I'm not basing too much of my personal worth on who and how many I can score in a single session, that is. Nothing at all to do with a less than perfect childhood and unending need for validation of my looks, I'm sure.

Still, I'd take one hard-core and amazingly passionate session over a dozen average ones any day—even if he isn't the most aesthetically pleasing of the pack, just as long as it isn't that saggy crypt keeper that's been cruising me all night. Nobody wants to be the last boy asked to dance after all.

Actually, come to think of it, some of my hottest fucks have been with average guys. Maybe they feel that they have to try harder to compensate or possibly they're just less concerned about how everything is looking and more focused on what feels fucking fantastic.

Mmm...good times.

Still feels weird that names are only exchanged at the end, if they are swapped at all; funny that we do quite intimate and personal things, without ever exchanging a word. It's not like I'm a chatterbox, but sometimes a little conversation wouldn't go astray. But that time in the changing room with that random pretty gym bunny, where we didn't say a single thing, was so incredibly hot.

When did I get here? Feels like I'm blending into one long, seedy blur of fun and heartbreak from my time here.

Ah, some of the most stunning examples of manhood, and those not quite so hot in the unforgiving lighting of the locker room...and Nic. He's still one of the hottest, sleaziest fucks I've ever had the pleasure to encounter, but also without doubt, the biggest cunt known to man.

Wow! Ten years since that time at the glory holes, doesn't feel that long ago. I still can't believe that he ended it all. I should have listened to everyone and just dumped his pert little ass when I had the chance. But I've always liked the bad boys.

Man, my body is aching just thinking about that sex. I guess all that anger and frustration had to go somewhere. Ah, that fine, fine line between love and hate that we crossed many, many times...whilst fucking like rabid wild animals. God I miss that, no matter how things ended, but maybe you just can't have that intensity with someone you like.

Nobody's ever quite matched that rawness of just wanting to destroy each other through fucking. I was so stupid to keep taking him back time and time again, but still...we did have something.

I should have known that it wouldn't end well. Still, I was surprised when I felt his hand in the middle of my back, right before I fell down the stairs to the sauna...breaking my neck. An accident, they thought, and of course Nic played the part of the grieving boyfriend so well.

It's not all that bad really; I can still actively participate after all. But being totally dependent on a walking stick wasn't something I'd particularly envisioned for my thirties. Not to mention years of soul-crushing and ridiculously painful physical therapy.

Sure there wasn't enough evidence to prosecute—only the

word of one hysterical queen over another's—but at least he's gone for good. Not even he's coldhearted enough to face the waves of collective hate constantly crashing down on him, from my nearest and dearest.

I guess I'm doomed to hang 'round here forever. On the upside, it's not like I'm alone in my affliction; thankfully some of them are even quite hot. It would be a total tragedy if I was stuck here forever with only dirty old men for company. God, I hope they don't turn this place into apartments.

Oh, hello...looks like he's changed his mind. Maybe he's got a thing for the handicapable; it takes all sorts, I guess. Besides, I'm never one to turn down a pity shag.

MONTGOMERY GYMNOS

Shane Allison

When I saw Bill at the movies last night, my heart dropped into my ball sac.

"Hey, man, how's it goin'?" Bill asked.

"Pretty good. How you doin'?"

"Can't complain. What are you here to see?"

"*Hugo*. I was trying to decide if I wanted to see that or *Breaking Dawn*." I lied through my teeth. I had my mind set on seeing the new Scorsese movie for a week. I hate that *Twilight* shit and I can't stand talentless Kristin "Boney Bitch" Stewart.

"I think you made the right decision," Bill grinned. He was dressed from his buzz-cut flattop to his black boots in cop garb, unlike the campus security getup he used to wear. Bill had moved up in the ranks.

"I think so, too." Bill still looked the same. He had aged slightly, lost some weight, but he was still fine as hell. And that cop uniform only made him hotter. I think someone told me he was working full-time at the Tallahassee Police Department.

"All right, Bill I'll see ya when I come out," I waved.

"Later, Shane."

Last time I saw him he almost caught me about to suck off this guy under the bathroom stalls in the Montgomery Gym showers back when he was a campus cop at Florida State University. Minutes before I was about to drop to my knees, I peered over my partition to see if the coast was clear and there in front of the door of the shower room stood two cops: Bill and this bald guy whom I had seen patrolling the campus. They both looked like they were not in the mood to take any shit. Bill didn't know who I was until I stepped out of the stall. Needless to say, I kept my cool.

"Bill, hey, how's it going?" I said timidly, as I sauntered up to one of the sinks to wash my hands.

"Shane," was all he said with this mean, militant look that ran across his face. I had no idea what the guy in the shitter next to me looked like until he eventually wandered out to join me at the sinks. He was cute with short, cinnamon-brown hair and a *phat* ass. Looking at him, I was pissed that we had been bothered only seconds before I was about to gobble this white boy's dick.

"What were you guys doing?" Bill asked.

"Nothing. I was just using the bathroom."

"So was I," the twink said. They looked at us knowing good and well that we weren't going to tell them what was really up. *Oh, I was just about to go down on this guy's dick before ya'll walked in.* Yeah, right. "We've been getting some complaints about suspicious behavior going on in here. You guys need to be careful." I was embarrassed that Bill suspected what I was doing or was about to do, but I had come out to him back in the day when we were ushers at this rat-infested movie theater. He was the only one who was cool with me. I did a three-month stent and hauled ass. I hated the married couple that ran the place. Bill and this guy Thaddeus were the only coworkers I talked to. I didn't even put in two weeks' notice. I didn't see Bill for six years before that day on campus.

I figured this old bitch who has an office located across from the gym showers was the one who called the po-po. She was always sitting at her desk watching like some big ol' black buzzard. They had no choice but to let us go being that they didn't catch us doing anything. I had already been warned by someone else who cruised to be careful, because the cops on campus were cracking down, coming in plainclothes, pretending to be students. They popped this guy just last week in the library shitters. I only go there as a last resort when I can't get any dick in the Bellamy bathrooms, which I usually frequent. They have glory holes in the stalls where guys stick their dicks through to get head. I sit on the other side where it's always best to give than to receive. I hardly ever like to get sucked. Damn, talking about this is making my dick stir.

The only thing that I couldn't stand about the Montgomery showers was that there was no time to recover if you were doing something and someone walked in. I had gotten pinched by the cops in the park a year before, so I wasn't going to take any chances. After Bill and his bald partner were done questioning us and had given us a warning, they let us go. The twink and I walked in different directions but met up later at a bench in front of the student union.

"Shit, that was close," I said.

"I know, right?"

"Had they come in seconds later, we would probably be on our way to jail," I told him.

"Yeah. You gotta be careful. I've heard the cops have been sniffing around."

"I bet it was that old lady who told on us," I said.

"What lady?"

"This old bitch that has an office across from the showers. Every time I go in, I see her just sitting there at her desk looking at who's going in and coming out. She's probably the one who called the cops."

"I've never seen her, but I'm glad I know that. I won't be going back there," he said.

"She's not there all the time though. You just gotta keep an eye out."

"Yeah, man, but the cops. If I get arrested, I could lose my scholarship; get my ass kicked out of school. My folks would kill me and then dig my ass back up once they found out what I got arrested for and kick my ass again."

This fool kept going on like I cared. I just wanted to suck his dick.

"Yeah, as long as you're careful, you won't get caught," I said.

"I don't think there's any such thing as being careful when you do that shit though."

He had a point.

"So we can um...go somewhere else if you want," I said.

"Naw, I'm pretty shaken up with what went down back there, man. I think I'm just gonna head out."

"Are you sure? I would love to suck your dick." The twink pulled away when I started to caress his thigh. He laughed like I was crazy to be so ballsy.

"Maybe another time, but thanks," he said. He walked off leaving me with a raging hard-on. *Well, take your ass on then. Fuck you!* I thought. I didn't think I would ever see him again, but being the tearoom queen that I am, I oughta know that they always come back. I got his dick after all in the ground-floor bathroom at Bellamy one afternoon. "Suck that cock," he kept saying.

Slurp.

Slurp.

Slurp.

I sucked until I made that white boy nut so fuckin' hard he got cum all over my jeans. He didn't know it was me until I stuck my head over the wall of my stall. He smiled when he saw that it was me and exited the bathroom. I never saw him again after that day. It's too bad, too. That was some good juicy dick. I love cruising on campus. College boys have primo boners.

I returned to Montgomery like a week later after I figured shit had died down. I kept watch for that old snitch-ass bitch that narced on me from the last time. If her office door was open, I knew she was perched at her usual spot. If it was closed, I knew she was out to lunch or had taken her ass home. The day that I went to go see what was up, her office door was closed. God wanted me to get some dick that day. When I walked in, all I heard was a shower running. The stalls were vacant. I occupied the one closest to the wall, the *giving* end. I waited for like an hour. The reverberation from the shower had gotten on my nerves. There I was half ass-naked on the toilet on hard and there wasn't a dick to be had. That's one of the things I hate about cruising. Shit can be hit or miss. I got bored just sitting there. My legs were starting to fall asleep. "Fuck this," I said, and pulled up my pants. "I'm going to Bellamy. I like it there better anyway."

I stood at the sink washing my hands when I spotted this image in the mirror. This guy was standing there behind me, booty-naked and wet. My eyes zeroed in on his fat donkey dick that hung between his tan-lined legs. He looked to be in his late twenties, early thirties maybe. All he wore was his glasses. He was balding. The hair he had left was thinning and blond. I had seen him before. I had the pleasure of sucking his pretty dick on a couple of occasions in the fifth floor toilet in Strozier Library. I think his name was John. A fake name I figured, but whatever. The windows were fogged with steam from the shower. I turned to face him. Shower water trickled along his chest and belly, beaded in his bushel of pubes, leaking like precum off the circumcised spout of his donkey dick. My glasses were starting to fog up like the set of windows above the showers.

"I hadn't seen you around. How are you?" John asked.

"What are you doing? You're gonna get caught." I couldn't stop cutting glances at his dick.

"It's cool. There hasn't been anyone around since I've been in here," he told me.

"Somebody still might come in though."

John was making me nervous standing there naked. He wasn't in the best of shape, but I don't mind a little chunk as long as it's in the right place, preferably the ass. I love to fuck and eat a nice bubble. John had a slight paunch, thick arms and thighs, and he had a little man-boob action coming in. John had a Seth Rogan physique before Seth Rogan went all Weight Watchers on a nigga. I was nervous as hell, but it didn't stop my dick from twitching in my jeans. I pulled my eyes from his thick cock long enough to ask, "So there hasn't been a lot of action going on in here?"

"I just got here. I haven't seen anybody." I figured if he had, he would be on his knees right now.

"I didn't know they still use these showers," I said. "I thought guys just come in here to change."

"I don't think they do, really. I was jogging and was going to go home to shower, but I didn't want to get my car seats all sweaty. I remembered these showers and came here."

He was torturing me. I was hungry for his dick. I took it in my hand and started to massage it as I ran my thumb across one of his nips. His dick was still warm from the shower, yet cool from the air that kissed it. I steered John's bulbous head to my lips and took his appendage into my mouth. His wet belly grazed against my glasses as I sucked.

Slurp.

Slurp.

Slurp.

I didn't care if we got caught or who saw us. All I could think about was sucking that dick. John pushed until his dick teased the rear of my throat.

"Let's hit the showers." I started to get undressed, stepping out of my sandals, dropping out of my shorts and drawers, peeling off my shirt. I followed John to the showers; pearls of water peppered his ass. I couldn't keep from looking at his taut booty. Both of our dicks were bone hard. Warm shower water pelted our bodies. We wrapped our fingers around each other's wet hard-ons.

"I want to rim your ass," I said.

"I've never had that done before, but I'm down."

I was eager to turn that ass out. John bent over. I traipsed a finger along his crack. I dropped to the balls of my knees. John's ass was point-blank to my face. The gym showers were thick with steam. John's treasure was exposed. I smeared my face in.

I licked, sucking at his cherry.

Give me that ass. John eased onto his elbows, face pressed into the shower floor. A bolt of shock and fear shot through my chest when I glanced up from John's ass to find Bill peering from behind the tile wall, jacking his dick that hung past the copper teeth of his zipper. Bill looked to be about seven and a half, maybe eight inches with a good amount of girth to his cop dick. He stood there in silence, watching us, watching me grind my face in between John's glutes. Nothing turns me on more than being watched. The more men the fucking better. His pale, skinhead of a partner wasn't with him. Too bad. I would have done them both. I waved him over as I kept eating ass. Bill started to get undressed. Shit, it was about to be on and poppin'. I watched him peel off his uniform. When he dropped the metallic holster on the floor from his slim waist, it startled John. Bill undid his shirt, exposing a bulletproof vest. More skin was steadily starting to show. Big powerful arms, a white cotton tee stretched over pectorals. I finger-teased John's hole as Bill stepped out of shoes and socks. A peach fuzz of hair was centered on his chest. Damn, he was fine. Don't know when the last time I had seen a body that looked that good. Bill crept along the shower floor in front of John, eager to take his appendage into his mouth.

I stood up off my knees. John was primed for fucking. I was starting to prune, so I shut off the shower. I straddled John, aiming my dick at his center. With a single thrust, it sank into his ass. Bill and I watched each other as we spit-roasted John from both ends. Bill's face flushed red. We were both close to shooting off. I knew Bill wouldn't hold out much longer, not with the deep-throating John was putting down on that cop cock.

Slurp.

Slurp.

I knew from experience that he wouldn't stop until he'd gotten that nut. The man was ravenous, so I wasn't surprised that he could keep up with us. The occasional moan and "Fuck, yeah!" echoed throughout the showers.

Damn, this some good ass.

Take this dick.

Take it.

Who knows how many dicks this bottom has taken up his ass? The backs of my thighs were on fire. Fuck, I couldn't hold out any longer. As I slid out, I jerked thick streams of nut across his pimpled ass.

Yeah.

Yeah.

Fuck yeah.

Fuckin' cum.

Bill continued to work his mouth.

"Yeah. Fuck his mouth."

"Suck that big fuckin' dick."

John started sucking Bill faster.

I looked up at Bill as he thrust his slab of cop dick in John's mouth.

"Fuck his face."

"Damn, man you can suck a dick."

"Here it comes," Bill said. Before another word rolled past my lips, Bill came.

Gulp.

Gulp.

"Take that cum," I said.

Bill eased his dick out of John's mouth. John lapped up the few drops of jizz from the spout of Bill's dick before collapsing on the floor. I was exhausted. Our dicks were limp against our thighs.

Damn that was hot.

Bill treated us like we weren't even there as he got dressed, buckling his shiny black holster back around his waist.

I stood naked before him.

"You want to um—do this on the reg?" I said in a cocky tone.

"They're gonna start cracking down hard on this place so you better stay out of here. Tell him to do the same. Better get dressed. The janitors will be by here soon to clean."

I put my clothes on, leaving John to shower off. The last time I saw him he was working at one of the bookstores on campus. I think about John sometimes, wondering if he has a lover, or has maybe converted to heterosexuality or is cruising some gym shower someplace.

Bill was outside in the lobby of the movie theater.

"How was it?"

"Good. Slow at first, but pretty good."

"My wife wants to see it, so we might try to make it by next week."

"You should. It's a cool movie," I said.

"Well, have a good night. It was good seeing you again," said Bill.

"You, too. Take care."

The following week I went to Montgomery Gym. They had remodeled the building, had turned the showers into a classroom. It was the end of an era. I left knowing that it was one of the hottest spots I had ever fucked in.

THE GAY DUDE

Gregory L. Norris

Tea-bagged

The first night Ben bailed on meeting them after work at the Home Run sports bar on an otherwise unremarkable hump day, Jason and Mikey didn't read much into things. When Ben blew them off again two nights later, they knew they had a situation: there was a problem in dude-dom.

"I smell something, and it stinks," said Jason, replaying the voice mail.

"*Yeah, sorry but I can't make it. Tell Mikey I'll catch you dudes later...*" Ben grumbled in a low voice, no further explanation offered.

"Really *stinks*."

Mikey gulped a hearty swig of the cheap tap bear sweating in his hand. "Then change your socks."

Jason shot the shorter dude a look. "You're the one with hairy toes."

"Yours are bigger; therefore they probably stink worse than mine."

"You know what they say about big feet."

"Big socks," Mikey fired back. "Stinky ones."

Jason punched Mikey's shoulder. "Shut the fuck up, dude."

"*Ow*!"

"Ow?" Jason narrowed his gaze in contemplation. "Dude's got some action going on—and he doesn't want us knowing about it."

Mikey leaned back in the seat, scratched at the crotch of his jeans and then his chin, now showing a decent five o'clock shadow at seven on a Friday night. "You think he's tea-bagging us?"

Jason nearly dropped the beer glass balanced on his lips and spit foam. "*Dude.*"

"What?" asked Mikey.

"Tea-bagged?"

"Yeah, you know, like he's stonewalling us, only worse. Tea-bagging."

"So, now Ben's dropping his balls on our noses in that famous gay bar in New York City?"

"What you and Ben do when I'm not around..."

"*Sand*bagging, dude," Jason said. "Though it does feel like Ben's been rubbing his sweaty sac all over our faces."

"Big hairy sac."

"Hairy and ripe, dude," Jason said. "Since when doesn't our good buddy Ben share the dirty deets when he's banging some sweet piece of ass?"

"Ben's only banged two that we know of since the divorce," said Mikey.

"That's two more than you."

"Hey," Mikey barked. "I get plenty of action."

"Yeah, of the tea-bag variety. I need to piss. Try not to suck on too many balls while I'm gone."

"Fuck you."

"You wish."

"No, that's Ben's job," Mikey chuckled.

Though clearly, the figurative responsibility joked about had been shirked, for their absent pal's focus had turned elsewhere.

Jason strutted into the men's head. The beer in his bladder and the sudden worry in his gut worked together to make each footfall heavier than it should have been. He passed the mirror over the double sinks en route to the nearest urinal, stole a glance at his reflection, winked at the handsome face gazing back. He feigned lightness for the last of the steps; with his neat athlete's haircut, arm muscles earned after a decade of working at the big-box hardware store in town and a lifetime of playing sports, he owned the walk.

Jason sauntered up to the men's head, unzipped, and unloaded, his lids half-closed. The men's room door creaked open. Movement teased his eyes at the periphery.

"Dude," said Mikey. "You think Ben's ashamed of us?"

Jason's eyes snapped fully open. "I don't know, but can we have this discussion when I'm not standing here with my dick hanging out?"

"Sure, I need to drop some coins in the fountain, anyway," said Mikey. He vanished behind a stall door.

"Ashamed?" Jason parroted. He shook out his meat, fondled his nuts, scowled.

"Or maybe our boy Benny's worried about his new chick getting itchy for something different. You know, competition from you and me."

Jason huffed, zipped. "There ain't much competition."

"Sure. You're the hot one, we all know that. I'm the cute one. And Ben's, you know, the smart one. Maybe he's afraid that hot or cute might trump smart."

A muffled explosion sounded from behind the stall door.

"*Hot*, anyway," said Jason.

Sweat glistened on his legs and arms, soaked his baseball cap and T-shirt. Jason flexed his toes and imagined the dampness in his ankle socks, the funky fragrance of his size-thirteen cross trainers, the ripeness of his balls. Jogging a couple of miles on a humid June morning left him dripping.

Jason's feet maneuvered him through the center of town, toward the beach. A couple of left turns took him to the corner of Atlantic Avenue and Cove. One way led toward the dunes and the water, while the other direction cut directly past Ben Rollins's place. The beach cottage had been in Ben's family for three generations. Ben, Jason and Mikey had played there as boys. Fucked there as men, too, Jason thought, a lusty smirk forming beneath that sheen of sweat. Holding onto the place had cost Ben a tidy sum following the divorce. And now a new piece of ass was on the scene, Jason was sure. Best he scope it out and make sure this one didn't end up taking what Ben had left to his name.

Wiping his face on the hem of his T-shirt, Jason turned in the direction of the cottage, his pulse galloping for reasons he couldn't at first identify.

A motorcycle was shoehorned into the driveway beside Ben's truck, one of those sports bikes with serious balls. Jason trotted up the walkway, a humid breeze whispering across his wet flesh.

"Can I help you, dude?" asked a man sitting in one of the beach chairs in the patio sheltered by fence and shrubbery.

Jason dug in his heels and turned toward the sound of the voice. Heat slammed into his back. In the tense second or so that followed, he drank in the image of the dude sitting where no dude should be: big, all muscle, sipping coffee, naked chest, guns inked with barbed wire and some military symbol complete with American flag—Army. The dog tags hanging around his neck confirmed that bit of intel. With his old jeans and bare feet, the dude with the pale blue eyes and dark-blond hair one length longer than service-short added up to create an alpha-male image that challenged even Jason's confidence.

"No, dude," he said, his mouth drying up. "Can I help *you*?"

"Nope, all good," the dude said, and sipped, his hand looking gigantic around the coffee cup, one that Jason recognized from a set that belonged to the cottage.

The two men eyeballed each other. Jason's new adversary offered a grin more snarl than actual smile that revealed a length of clean white teeth. Jason matched it with a similar expression.

"Ben home?"

"You a friend of his?" the dude asked.

"Yeah, dude, you?"

"Yup," he said. "He's in the shower."

The dude tipped his chin toward the front door, a gesture as arrogant and cocky as it was basic in its delivery. Like Jason needed this ripped prick's permission to enter—*hell*, Jason had rubbed out enough loads into gym socks under that roof to have marked the place with a kind of territorial ownership.

He offered a tip of his chin in response and marched up the three concrete steps inlaid with seashells collected long ago on the nearby beach. Through the door. Into the cottage's living room, with its flat-screen TV over the mantle, and an even more recent addition: a pair of beat-up Army boots beside the sofa.

"Yo, Marcus," Ben called from the kitchen.

A moment later, Ben Rollins wandered into view, his hair wet, his body naked, his dick ticktocking half-hard ahead of him.

"Fuck, dude, put that thing away before you poke out a fucking eyeball!"

Shock washed over Ben, obvious in the redness that rose up the top of his chest to stain his throat scarlet. He grabbed a gaming magazine off the sofa and covered his junk with the image of some anime character sporting a neon-green Mohawk.

"What the fuck, dude?" Ben bellowed.

Jason folded his arms. "That's what me and Mikey would like to know."

"Nothing, man." Ben straightened, attempting a casual stance, his cock and nuts barely covered.

"Nothing? Then why are you blowing us off, dude? And who the fuck is that G.I. Joe out there?"

Ben cast a nervous glance in the direction of the front door. "Marcus? He's just a friend."

Jason swept an arm, wagged his fingers, creating a physical question. Before he could add actual words, Marcus shuffled into the cottage. "Hey," he said.

"Hey," Ben answered and then cleared his throat. "Marcus, this is my good pal Jason. Jason, Marcus."

Marcus offered a hand, huge like the dude's feet. Jason relaxed his questioning fingers and shook, the pressure from each dude's grip strong enough to snap the bones of lesser men. No words were spoken for what seemed to Jason a good deal longer than the few actual seconds during which alpha faced off against alpha.

The new dude blinked first. "Listen, I've got to motor. Catch you later at the Pavilion?" he said to Ben, who was still standing with his dick concealed behind glossy print.

"Call you."

The two men exchanged a knowing look, something not lost on Jason. Then Marcus pulled a T-shirt and the pair of run-in combat boots from beside the sofa. The house shook when the sports bike pulled out and gunned it down Atlantic Ave.

Jason pinned Ben through narrowed eyes. "Who's that military motherfucker?"

"I told you."

"Nuh-uh, no you didn't."

"Yes, I did—he's a friend."

"I don't know him."

"College friend. In town for a week, needed a place to stay."

"Oh," said Jason.

The explanation seemed reasonable enough, so he bought it. As Mikey was always fond of saying, Ben was the one with the brains.

"Mikey thinks you're tea-bagging."

Ben paled. "What?"

"For crissakes, dude—would you put some clothes on!"

Rub-a-Dub-Dub, Four Dudes in a Tub

"College buddy? Which college buddy?"

Jason unapologetically scratched at his nuts with one hand, bounced the basketball with the other. "The one who looks like Thor, God of Thunder—only with a military haircut. How the fuck do I know?"

He scooped the basketball over his shoulder. The ball circled the rim and dropped through into Mikey's waiting hands.

"So it isn't some new chick?"

"Not unless the chick has guns like Schwarzenegger from back in the eighties and balls bigger than the one you're traveling with."

Mikey dribbled, maneuvered around Jason's reaching hands and shot. The ball bounced out. Mikey recovered and slam-dunked it into the net. "He gonna meet us tonight?"

"I dunno—he and his new best pal Marcus are supposed to

connect later at some place called the Pavilion. Ever hear of it?" Mikey hadn't. "Something stinks."

"Here we go again. Take a shower, dude."

"You take the shower! And then meet me at my place, six o'clock."

"Why don't I just see you at the bar?"

"Because we're getting to the bottom of this. *Tonight*."

The car approached.

"Get down. *Down*," Mikey blathered.

"Dude, I'm six-three. This is as down as I get," Jason said.

Mikey poked back up from the passenger's seat. "Was that Ben?"

"Yeah, it was. And lose the ridiculous disguise."

Jason threw his truck into drive and gunned the gas. Mikey dropped his hoodie's hood and removed his sunglasses.

They followed Ben out of the neighborhood and tracked him past the dunes, toward the beach and, several miles later, to a squat gray stone building sitting by itself beneath a row of tall pines. The only identifying sign on the place read: PAVILION.

"This is it. What the fuck is this joint?"

"How the fuck should I know?" Mikey countered.

Jason drove past, circled back and pulled into the lot. A dozen cars, Ben's truck among them, were parked beneath the pines. The dense canopy of branches cast an artificial twilight over the building, which seemed a thousand miles away from anything familiar, not a mere five down the road.

"Now what?" asked Mikey.

Jason shrugged. Before he could think of an appropriate answer, a sports car pulled in beside them, its driver a goateed beach bum, Jason assumed, according to the dude's tan. The bum tipped his chin at them in greeting, that universal gesture between men who've just met that turns all males into instant pals.

"You dudes new?" the bum asked.

"Uh," Jason stammered, glanced at Mikey. "Sure."

The bum smiled, winked. "Fucking-A. See you inside."

The man exited his car, walked off, his steps confident, and vanished inside the building.

"Friendly dude," Mikey said.

"Yeah, sure," Jason agreed.

"Maybe this place is like a gym."

"Ben was looking fairly buff when I saw him this morning," Jason said.

"I thought you said he was bare-assed and swinging dick?"

Jason bopped the shorter dude across the top of his head. "Come on."

They got out of the truck and followed the beach bum—and Ben—into the Pavilion.

A wall of steamy air ripe with the sweaty scent of other dudes slammed into Jason.

"I think you're right about the place being a gym. It's funkier in here than the locker room where I work out."

Mikey waved a hand in front of his face, clearing the fog enough to make out a check-in counter, where a dude was handing out towels. Cute led Hot over.

"Welcome to the Pavilion, gentlemen," the dude said.

"Oh, we're not—" Mikey began, until Jason shoved him forward and the sentence went unfinished.

The willowy dude at the counter coughed to clear his throat. "Lockers to the left, baths to your right. Please make sure to follow all the rules, which are posted in all of the rooms. The

Pavilion is not responsible for lost or stolen articles, so it's recommended that you pay for a locker."

"Fine," Jason said, and paid.

They stripped down to just their sneakers, towels wrapped around their waists, and journeyed into the mysterious realm to the right of the lockers and counter.

"It's some kind of steam room," said Mikey. "Phew, I already feel like I've lost five pounds."

"That's because you're a sweaty little monkey-boy," said Jason.

"Shut the fuck up, Lurch."

Mikey walked ahead into a labyrinth of alcoves and doors leading to smaller, private, steam-filled rooms, many of them closed to prying eyes. The hiss of running water telegraphed that, somewhere in the maze, showers ran in a continuous cycle.

"Fuck, I think this place is making my balls melt," said Jason. "Seriously, they're swinging halfway down to my ankles."

"Don't trip over them. We still need to find Ben, dude, and figure out what the fuck he's doing here. What *we're* doing here when all three of us could be at Home Run chugging down some cold ones instead of making our bags sag."

The throat of the labyrinth opened wider, becoming a main room with wooden benches set stadium-style around a central cauldron of steaming rocks. Human shapes were silhouetted in that brimstone landscape, only they didn't appear to only be soaking up the steam.

"Dude, what's that smell?" asked Mikey.

"Balls, I think," Jason replied.

One of the bodies rose from the bench and approached. As the dude drew closer, his features solidified—the beach bum from the parking lot.

"About time, pal," the bum said to Jason. "I've been going crazy waiting for a taste. You, and your little buddy."

The man flashed a smirk at Mikey.

And then he reached beneath Jason's towel and groped his sweaty junk.

Shouts thundered through the labyrinth and echoed off walls. Doors opened. Behind one of the nearest to the commotion, Ben appeared, again naked, his dick standing stiffly as fingers squeezed down on the root and a set of lips gobbled the head.

"Jason?" Ben gasped. "*Mikey*? Oh, fuck!"

Mikey ceased howling and peered into the room. The lips so skillfully slobbering over Ben's cock belonged to Marcus.

Ben stood awkwardly and yanked his bone from the other man's mouth.

"*Dude*," said Jason. He folded his arms, temporarily forgetting that his towel lay untold yards behind them, somewhere in that soupy no-man's land, likely still in the hands of the beach bum who'd gone fishing beneath it for a feel of Jason's steam-loosened nuts.

"*Dude*," Ben answered.

"*Dude*?" asked Mikey, eyes wide.

Marcus rose from his knees, his erection swinging out from his magnificent, naked body. "*Dudes!*"

"I've seen more of your hairy Johnson today than in the past five years, man," Jason admonished, arms folded, the defensive posture of his body language impossible to misread.

"Why five?" asked Marcus.

Ben leaned closer. "He and I tag-teamed the stripper at my bachelor party."

"Did your dicks touch?"

Ben nodded. "And our sacs."

"Shut up," Jason barked. "You swore—"

"You never told me about that," Mikey said.

"You'll have to tell me more about that," said Marcus to Ben, his lusty smirk widening. His impressive dick, the biggest one bouncing in their naked dude-huddle, pulsed.

"Where was I?" asked Mikey.

"Shut up. All of you, just *shut the fuck up*," said Jason. "And you...old college pal? My asshole, dude."

Ben locked eyes with Jason. "So which is it gonna be? Do you want me to shut up or talk?"

"I want you to come clean. About this...*him*."

"Him?" Ben parroted. "He's just about the best thing that's ever happened to me."

Jason dismissed the statement with a sigh. "What?"

"Maybe it's better if we show the dudes," said Marcus.

The big dude lowered to his knees in front of Ben. Opening wide, Marcus sucked Ben's dick back between his lips.

Shocked, Jason and Mikey watched, their mouths open, their dicks responding in the only manner possible. Marcus sucked. Ben moaned and unloaded. Marcus stood, fresh wetness glistening on his cheek. Without shame or apology, he and Ben kissed.

"No, no, *no*," said Jason. "This can't be real. Who are you? What did you do with the real Ben?"

"It's me, dude," said Ben.

Marcus licked his mouth. "Oh, yeah, that tastes like the real Ben, for sure."

Jason marched out of the steam room and through the Pavilion's front entrance. He was halfway across the parking lot before he realized he was only wearing sneakers.

* * *

"So, dude, you're...gay?"

Ben shifted uncomfortably in his chair, unwilling or unable to meet Jason's gaze. Until that moment, his beer glass had sat untouched. Ben drained it in one deep swig before answering. "I don't know. I don't think so, but...all I do know, dude, is that I've never felt complete until now. Until I met Marcus. After the divorce...it sounds crazy, but I've never been happier."

"I can't blame you, especially the way that dude hummed all over your bone," said Mikey.

Jason shot Mikey a look. Cute shrank. "What? What?"

Jason again faced Ben. "And you couldn't come to us? Dude, you're my best pal. You and nut sac over here." He aimed a thumb at Mikey. "What we've been through together, what we've done..."

"What *you* two dudes did, not me. I wasn't invited to join in on the stag party tag-team action," said Mikey.

"You're missing the point," said Jason.

"The point is, okay—now you know the truth. You know all of it. You know about me and Marcus. I don't know what he and I are, but we're together. Deal with it."

Ben delivered the challenge in a way that left no room for debate, showing serious balls. Saying nothing, respecting the dude's sac, Jason extended his hand across the table. Ben accepted, shook, and then repeated the gesture with Mikey. Following the shake, Ben offered his hand, palm down, Three Musketeers–style.

"Don't know what I'm more jealous of," Mikey said, covering Ben's hand. Jason completed the ritual, all for one, one for all. "The stag party or that you're getting such excellent head."

"Head to *toe*," Ben said after pulling free.

"Toe?" This came from Jason. "He licks *feet*?"

"He licks everything. Oh, fuck, Marcus is the best."

"I can't believe it," said Jason. "Even though I saw it with my own fucking eyes, I still can't believe that dude's *gay*."

The Gay Dude

They met at the Pavilion, a local hangout for gay dudes, Ben confessed. He'd learned of the place by doing an online search during the lowest of his recent low and lonely nights. The Pavilion was right in their backyard. It had taken him a week, Ben claimed, to get up the nuts to actually go inside.

Marcus approached the table dressed in a white T-shirt and jeans, old combat boots and older leather jacket, motorcycle helmet in hand. "There room for one more?"

Ben glanced at Jason and then Mikey. Though grim-faced, the two dudes nodded.

"Sure," Ben said.

Marcus took the seat in reverse, assuming the classic stance of cowboys, outlaws and tough guys. "So, we all cool now?"

"Not quite," said Jason. "There are one or two more things we need to get straight. Correct, I mean."

"Fine, shoot. Name them, I mean."

Jason deferred to Mikey. "Well, for a start, this has always been a *dude-dom* of three."

"A dude-dom?" Marcus chuckled.

"Work with me, dude. Yeah, three. There's the smart one—"

He pointed at Ben.

"The hot one."

Jason straightened and flashed a cocky grin.

"And the cute one." Mikey aimed both thumbs at his chest.

"Well, I'm fairly intelligent," said Marcus.

"Trust me, he is—three tours in the desert, communications

expert." Ben made a fist and offered his knuckles to Marcus, who then tapped them.

"Don't read anything into this," Jason said. "But you're definitely smoking-hot."

"Thanks, buddy."

"At least you're not cute," said Mikey.

"Marcus rescued a bunch of puppies over there, had them brought over here, made sure they all got new homes."

"Oh man, dammit," said Mikey. "It doesn't get any cuter than rescuing puppies from war! We definitely have a problem in dude-dom, dude."

"We do?"

Mikey eyed Marcus, made a circular motion with his finger. "Yes, because what makes this all work is that we each own something different from the others. You've got a whole lot of everything, so it don't work anymore. It'll all crash down on top of our dicks, dude. The dude-dom's gonna collapse."

Marcus considered the statement. "I don't want the dude-dom falling apart, but I think I have a solution on how to make it work. Because I really like Ben, and I want to hang out with his good buddies—the hot one and the cute one."

"What's your plan?" Jason asked.

"You're the hot dude, he's the cute dude, and Ben's the smart dude. Simple. Just think of me as the gay dude."

"The gay dude," Mikey laughed while handing a cold bottle to Marcus. "I don't believe you're gay. Dude, if I had your looks, your guns...fuck, your *dick*, I'd be getting laid every night."

"I am getting laid every night," Marcus said coolly, tipping a glance toward the beach cottage's front door, indicating Ben sitting outside on the patio with Jason, the two dudes presently in the middle of a good laugh straight out of the old days.

"Yeah, right. I just meant—"

"You meant with women. I tried that, realized I'm into dudes. Being gay doesn't make me any less of a man."

Marcus took a chug. The American flag tattoo around his biceps swayed majestically in an invisible breeze.

Mikey choked down a dry swallow. "No, it doesn't. Dude, do you...?"

Marcus eyed him, his lips detaching from around the longneck's opening. "Do I what?"

In a lower voice, Mikey said, "I've never seen Ben this happy before. I figure that you're really good at making a dude feel like a king."

"No complaints."

Fresh sweat broke across Mikey's forehead. "So, are you interested in servicing other dudes? Meaning me...'cause I could really use some of that kind of happy. So long as you know that I'm not interested in blowing you back. Maybe I could give you a tug, yank on your balls a little..."

The door opened, and Jason and Ben returned to find Marcus scowling and Mikey looking like he'd just buried a body.

"So," Jason asked Marcus, corner of the mouth. His gaze darted toward the kitchen, where Ben and Mikey were gathering snacks to accompany the latest round of beers. "This thing you got with Ben...is it exclusive?"

"Exclusive?"

Jason leaned closer. "I gotta assume you know what you're doing, the way you gobbled down Ben's dick in that sweat shop, right to the nuts. Ben says you're amazing, that you're into feet, of all things. *Feet*! I've got a big ole pair on me...they get funky when I work out, or after I've been on them for a ten-hour shift at work. Dude, I'm a manager at the big home goods superstore out on

Route 16...it's tough guy work. I get my share of pussy, as you can imagine, but a dude can never kick back for enough skilled head, am I right? I'm sure you know. And I've always wondered what it would be like to have my toes sucked on. So if you like feet—"

"I like *Ben's* feet."

Ben and Mikey sauntered back into the living room, where the baseball game played on the flat-screen and the conversation between Jason and Marcus shorted out, torn uncleanly down the middle.

"What's going on here?" Ben asked.

Marcus grabbed one of the longnecks in Ben's grasp. "Ask the hot dude—and the cute dude, too, while you're at it."

Jason and Mikey exchanged guilty looks.

"Spill, dudes," Ben grumbled.

Jason took a beer, popped the cap, and gulped down a hearty swig. "I was just wondering if Marcus had any interest in spreading the wealth around, that's all. You know, like at the stag party."

"Well, I'm shocked. Ashamed," Mikey said. "*Dude.*"

"You've got no room to talk," said Marcus. "Both of my new buds wanted to know if it's okay to pass my mouth around."

Ben tipped his eyes from Jason to Mikey and then Marcus before again shooting looks at his two buddies. "No, it's not. *Get your own gay dudes*!"

Ben closed the door. "Now that we've settled that issue and everything's back to being normal..."

Hands tucked in his pockets, Marcus rocked back and forth on the balls of his feet. "Go easy on them."

"I always do. And in the meanwhile..."

Ben wrapped an arm around Marcus's waist and drew him into a playful embrace.

"Yes?" Marcus asked around kisses.

"You up for staying the night?"

Marcus backed Ben toward the bedroom. "Why do you think I spent all those years in uniform?"

"To keep America safe?"

"That, and to defend my right to suck your dick."

He pushed Ben onto the bed, removed his sneakers and socks. Marcus lifted Ben's left foot and licked the sweat from between each toe before moving on to the right and showing it similar affection. Spit glistened. Then Marcus moved higher, unbuckling Ben's belt, lowering his zipper. Pants came down, exposing black boxer-briefs beneath. Ben's dick stood at its fullest mast, a wet spot expanding across its crown.

"I like those dudes," Marcus said.

"Dude, can we not talk about them right now?"

"Deal, dude," Marcus chuckled.

Boxer-briefs joined jeans in the growing pile of discarded clothes beside the bed.

"Suck my dick, dude," Ben moaned.

"Not yet."

Marcus scattered slow, teasing licks over Ben's inner thighs and balls. Lower, his tongue inched toward asshole territory. Once there, Marcus feasted.

"You're fucking incredible, dude," Ben moaned.

Licking his lips, Marcus said, "I sure fucking am."

Proving it yet again in actions as well as words, Marcus sucked Ben's dick all the way down.

"You're back," the dude at the counter said to Jason.

"Yeah, dude," Jason grumbled.

A few minutes later, he emerged from the Pavilion's lockers wrapped in a towel. Getting to the steam room took herculean effort. Time slowed, as did Jason's shuffling feet. But his dick, stiff behind the towel, urged him onward. Fucker had been hard for days, ever since learning the truth about Ben and Marcus, Jason guiltily admitted to himself during the inner monologue between front desk and baths.

Halfway through the labyrinth, he bumped into Mikey.

"Dude," said Jason.

"Dude?" Mikey fired back. "What are you doing here?"

Jason folded his arms. "I could ask you the very same thing."

Mikey's glazed expression toughened. "I don't know."

"You seen Ben?"

"Nope."

"What about Marcus?"

A shadow stirred the steam. Another man moved through the passageway, toward the heart of the labyrinth. It was the beach bum.

"Hey," said Jason, tipping his chin.

"Hey, yourself."

"About the other day. Sorry, dude."

The beach bum shuffled to a stop. "Sorry that I handled your hog?"

"No, not about that part. Sorry I scooted."

The beach bum grinned. "Apology accepted," he said and continued past the two men, toward the benches. Right as the swampy mist engulfed him, the dude turned around. "Come on, tough guy. I've waited long enough to suck that hot dick of yours."

Jason coughed, swallowed, and nearly tripped over his own huge feet while hurrying forward.

"You, too, dude," the beach bum said to Mikey. "Get your dick over here. Fuck, you're cute."

ABOUT THE AUTHORS

MICHAEL BRACKEN's short fiction has been published in *Best Gay Romance 2010, Beautiful Boys, Biker Boys, Black Fire, Boy Fun, Boys Getting Ahead, Country Boys, Freshmen, The Handsome Prince, Homo Thugs, Hot Blood, The Mammoth Book of Best New Erotica 4, Men, Muscle Men, Teammates* and many other anthologies and periodicals.

ERIC DEL CARLO's erotica has appeared with Circlet Press, Loose Id, Ravenous Romance, Cleis Press and other venues. He also writes science fiction and fantasy, appearing in such publications as *Asimov's* and *Strange Horizons*, and is the coauthor of the mystery novel *NO Quarter.* Check out ericdelcarlo.com for more info.

HEIDI CHAMPA has been published in numerous anthologies including *College Boys, Like Magnets We Attract, Skater Boys* and *Hard Working Men.* Short stories can be found at Dreamspinner Press, Ravenous Romance and Torquere Press. Find more online at heidichampa.blogspot.com.

LANDON DIXON's writing credits include *Boy Fun, Who's Your Daddy?, The Sweeter the Juice, Big Holiday Packages, Best of Both, Brief Encounters, Hot Daddies, Gym Buddies & Buff Boys, In Plain View, Hot Jocks, Uniforms Unzipped, Black Dungeon Masters, Ultimate Gay Erotica, and Best Gay Erotica*.

JEFF FUNK's stories have appeared in *Straight Guys, Frat Boys, Brief Encounters, Hard Working Men, Skater Boys* and *Hard Hats*. He's the author of *Bad Boy, Curious, Rascal, Stranger* and *Midnight Reader.*

JIMI GONINAN is an Australian writer, happily living in Paris with his French husband and cats. He writes a popular blog for *Têtu*, the premier French gay lifestyle magazine, as well as contributing to similar publications around the globe.

T. HITMAN is the *nom-de-porn* of a professional writer whose short fiction was featured monthly in issues of *Men*, *Freshmen*, *Torso* and other fine glossy gay men's newsstand magazines until the ax fell on them in 2010. For five years, he also wrote the *Unzipped* Web Review column.

ROSCOE HUDSON is a creative writer and academic. His stories have appeared in many publications, including *Best Gay Erotica 2012*, published by Cleis Press. He lives in Chicago.

SHAUN LEVIN is the author of *Seven Sweet Things* and *A Year of Two Summers*. His more recent books include *Trees at* *a Sanatorium* and *Snapshots of The Boy*. He teaches creative writing and devises Writing Maps (writingmaps.com).

GREGORY L. NORRIS is the author of the recent monster-sized collection of stories short and long, *The Fierce and Unforgiving Muse: Twenty-Six Tales from the Terrifying Mind of Gregory L. Norris* by Evil Jester Press. Visit him on Facebook and online at gregorylnorris.blogspot.com.

ROB ROSEN, author of the critically acclaimed novels *Sparkle: The Queerest Book You'll Ever Love, Divas Las Vegas, Hot Lava, Southern Fried,* and *Queerwolf,* has had short stories featured in more than 170 anthologies. Please visit him at www.therobrosen.com.

TROY STORM has had over two hundred erotic short stories published under various pseudonyms in *Penthouse*, *Playgirl*, *Honcho*, *Inches* and many other magazines that no longer exist. His stories also appear in numerous anthologies such as Shane Allison's *Brief Encounters* for Cleis Press.

RAFAELITO V. SY (rafsy.com) was born in Manila. He earned his BA from Tufts University and his MFA in creative writing from Cornell University. His 2005 novel, *Potato Queen*, is about the segregationist relationship between Asians and Caucasians in the San Francisco gay community.

T. R. VERTEN is the author of the erotic novella *Confessions of Rentboy*, published by Republica Press. The best place to find her is on Twitter @trepverten where she talks about hot boys, her cats and what's for dinner.

C. C. WILLIAMS's works appear in such collections as *Frat Boys*, *Brief Encounters*, *Best Gay Romance 2012*, *Wild Boys* and *The Love That Never Dies*. When not critiquing cooking show contestants, he's at work on several projects. You're invited to find out more at ccwilliamsonline.net.

THOM WOLF (thom-wolf.blogspot.com) has written two erotic novels *The Chain* and *Words Made Flesh*. Two short-story collections, *Bedtime Stories* and *Body Language*, have recently been published as e-books. He lives in a small town in County Durham, England and is working on his third novel.

LOGAN ZACHARY (loganzachary2002@yahoo.com) is an author of mysteries, short stories, and over fifty erotica stories. He lives in Minneapolis, MN with his partner, Paul, and his dog, Ripley, who runs the house. His new book is *Calendar Boys*.

ABOUT THE EDITOR

Award-winning editor **SHANE ALLISON** is the proud editor of a dozen smoking-hot gay erotica-themed anthologies published by Cleis Press including *Hot Cops; Backdraft; Frat Boys;* The Gaybie award-winning *College Boys; Brief Encounters: 69 Hot Gay Shorts; Cruising: Gay Erotic Fiction; Middle Men; Afternoon Pleasures: Gay Erotica for Gay Couples; Hard Working Men* and *Straight Guys*. He has had stories grace the pages of such anthologies as *Best Black Gay Erotica, Best Gay Erotica 2007, 2008, 2009, 2010* and 2011, *Country Boys, Leathermen, I Like to Watch* and a gay *pornucopia* of others. He is at work on his first novel and continues to work on bringing you a steady stream of mind-blowing, toe-curling dick literature like the anthology you now hold in your hands. Shane lives in Tallahassee, Florida.

More from Shane Allison

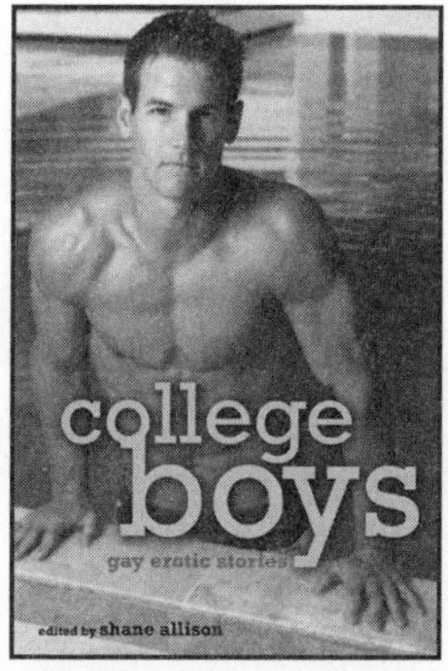

College Boys
Gay Erotic Stories
Edited by Shane Allison
First feelings of lust for another boy, all-night study sessions, the excitement of a student hot for a teacher...is it any wonder that college boys are the objects of fantasy the world over?
ISBN 978-1-57344-399-9 $14.95

Hot Cops
Gay Erotic Stories
Edited by Shane Allison
"From smooth and fit to big and hairy... it's like a downtown locker room where everyone has some sort of badge."—*Bay Area Reporter*
ISBN 978-1-57344-277-0 $14.95

Frat Boys
Gay Erotic Stories
Edited by Shane Allison
ISBN 978-1-57344-713-3 $14.95

Brief Encounters
69 Hot Gay Shorts
Edited by Shane Allison
ISBN 978-1-57344-664-8 $15.95

Backdraft
Fireman Erotica
Edited by Shane Allison
"Seriously: This book is so scorching hot that you should box it with a fire extinguisher and ointment. It will burn more than your fingers." —*Tucson Weekly*
ISBN 978-1-57344-325-8 $14.95

Afternoon Pleasures
Erotica for Gay Couples
Edited by Shane Allison
ISBN 978-1-57344-658-7 $14.95

Hard Working Men
Gay Erotic Fiction
Edited by Shane Allison
ISBN 978-1-57344-406-4 $14.95

*** Free book of equal or lesser value. Shipping and applicable sales tax extra.**
Cleis Press • (800) 780-2279 • orders@cleispress.com
www.cleispress.com